RING FOR A NURSE

Gorgeous Dr Angus Moray is the talk of
Beatties, both for his absent-mindedness
and his habit of taking attractive nurses
away for the weekend in his camper-van!
Nurse Petula Howard isn't certain what he
gets up to—but whatever it is, *she's* not
going with him . . .

CHAPTER ONE

'MUST YOU burst in like that?' Nurse Petula Howard hid her face under the bedclothes and tried to turn away from the sudden burst of light.

'You *did* ask me to call you, remember?' Dulcie walked over to the drawn curtains and flung them aside with a kind of relentless enjoyment. 'Lovely day for December,' she said, cheerfully. Rain spattered the window and a tired and very bare tree gave no hint of colour out in the grey light of a cold, wet morning.

'I should have known it was no good sleeping for two hours, but I was half dead when I came off duty last night. Is it really time for the lecture?'

'You have exactly ten minutes to get dressed and to run up to Grey Stones,' Dulcie laughed. 'I thought that would make you move! Actually, you have fifteen minutes,' she conceded, with conscious generosity.

'I feel really awful.' Petula shivered, although the room in the nurses' home was well heated and comfortable. She reached for her dressing-gown and yawned her way to the bathroom, slapped her face with cold water and pulled a comb through her light brown hair. Three months on night duty had done little to get her accustomed to the change of

5

routine and the unnatural hours of working and sleeping.

She put on her uniform without being aware that she did so. Every movement was automatic, the habit of nearly nine months' training at the Princess Beatrice Hospital in London and the seemingly endless routine of changing to go on duty, changing when she came off and changing back again if she was on a split shift or attending important lectures.

'Cap,' said Dulcie and handed a white-headed pin to the sleepy girl. 'Come on, we'll just make it.' She seized her cloak and handed the one on the chair to Petula, who accepted it without a word and draped it round her slender shoulders as if wrapping herself in a blanket. 'Snap out of it, Pet! You can't go to sleep in his lecture!'

The sharp, damp air was reviving and Petula took deep breaths as they almost ran up the slope to the old grey house on the hill which was used for the preliminary training school of Beatties, as the hospital was called by staff and patients.

At one time, the PTS had been within the grounds of the old hospital, but it had been destroyed by fire a few years ago. Only the staff who had been working at Beatties for many years could remember the place and Grey Stones was now accepted as the full-time centre for the education and examination of nurses in training.

'Why does the stupid man want to lecture this morning? I thought he was to give three classes after Christmas when we are in Block,' Petula grumbled.

'Sister Tutor wasn't very pleased when she heard that he wanted to do one now, but I believe he has to go away after Christmas for a week and will have time for only two of the three,' Dulcie explained.

'He doesn't care that he's putting out the whole schedule and almost killing one frail and dedicated nurse into the bargain!' Dulcie smiled and knew that her friend was now fully awake. The fact that she was grumbling was a certain sign that she was coming back to life.

'You, frail? Just because you would fit into a pint mug doesn't mean you aren't tough.' Dulcie pushed her friend inside the wide entrance and pulled off her cloak, hanging it with her own on one of the metal hooks inside the hall. Already, there were seven other cloaks hanging in a neat row of navy blue and red wool, as well as a few raincoats and duffles belonging to the nurses living in while they went through the first stages of their training.

'Good. Looks as if we beat him to it. No male garment sullies this female sanctum,' said Dulcie. 'Where are you going? It's two minutes to the hour. You know he hates starting late.'

'I can't help it, Dulcie, I forgot to go to the loo. You go in and save a seat for me, preferably in the back row. I won't be long.'

Petula disappeared into the cloakroom behind the coat-racks and Dulcie hesitated, wondering if she should wait. But the main door opened and a tall, spare figure stood on the mat, shaking rain from a padded raincoat and opening and shutting a large umbrella several times, sending clouds of spray on to the chairs lining the wall. Dulcie slipped past him into the lecture room, silently praying that Petula would be in the room before the door was closed. Sister Tutor came out into the hall, pursed her lips when she saw the damp chairs and then smiled bleakly. But the man, who now rubbed his hands together and thrust back the thick auburn hair, was oblivious to any coolness apart from the chill of the weather.

'All ready, Sister?' The voice was warm and brisk and the slight Scottish accent might, in other circumstances, have been attractive. Unfortunately, Sister was in no mood to be charmed by a doctor who upset her programme and whose lecture would be wasted if not taught within the context of his other two. And the other two were to be given after Christmas, when the girls had settled into the month in Block.

'All ready, Dr Moray,' she said and led the way into the lecture room. The murmur of voices faded as the doctor took his place on the slightly raised dais at one end of the room and regarded the small audience with a penetrating stare. They waited in silence, sensing that this was a man who controlled any situation in which he found himself, whether it was dealing with a crisis on the wards or teaching a bunch of young women who thought they had better things to do than to attend an extra lecture in their own time.

He glanced at his watch, and as if to confirm the fact that it was precisely eleven a.m. the church clock from down the hill began to strike the hour.

'Right. Are you all here?' He glanced round at the now attentive faces and at the blank pages of opened notebooks before each of them, and a faint smile lit his vivid blue eyes. 'I haven't time to waste, so we'll begin at once,' he said. 'What do you know about Parkinson's disease?'

Two of the nurses sighed gently. It was going to be *that* kind of a lecture, was it? They were quite prepared to sit absorbing knowledge and to watch the rather interesting face of the best-looking man they had seen for a long time, but he was going to make them work!

One of the eager beavers made the right replies and he nodded. But he stopped her before she could tell him what went onto a neurological examination tray, switching his attention to a student who had hoped that she would be unseen behind the plump, tall girl who blocked her view. She faltered and answered badly and the smile died from his eyes, a hint of impatience taking its place. He turned to Dulcie, who had not worked on a medical ward yet, and found that she was better but her knowledge was textbook only.

'I had hoped that they would know the rudiments of the subject, Sister,' he said.

'They are only at the end of the first year, Dr

Moray,' she pointed out mildly. 'They were hoping to learn about it from you.'

'But this is the elementary stuff! I'm used to teaching medical students and I would have thought that this class would have known about simple examinations.'

'I think that you will find the average medical student knows even less about examination procedures until they have met the cases in the ward,' Sister replied. 'Some of these girls have yet to work in a medical ward and have not had to lay up for neurological cases since PTS. This *is* your first set of lectures for the nursing staff, isn't it?'

He flushed, and she went on soothingly, 'Dr O'Flyn used to take them, and he didn't expect too much until the nurses had gained some practical experience.'

Her mild tones seemed to annoy him. 'Dr O'Flyn has retired, Sister. *I* am taking these lectures now, heaven help me.' He tried to smile but heard a slight snigger from the back row and his brow darkened. The door was opened timidly and Nurse Petula Howard came into the room, her normally pale face pink and her manner apologetic.

'What do you want?' he said, and she looked as if she wanted to vanish through a crack in the floor-boards.

'I've come for the lecture, Doctor. I'm sorry, I didn't think I was late.'

'Three minutes late,' he said briskly. 'Please remember that I am allergic to latecomers to my lectures.'

Petula murmured a further apology and sank into the seat next to Dulcie, glad to be away from those probing blue eyes. But she wasn't free from his attention.

'And now you have condescended to join us, Nurse . . . ?'

'Nurse Howard,' she said.

'Well, Nurse Howard, we were just trying to find out if anyone knew anything at all here.' She wilted under the intent gaze. 'Now, tell me what, if anything, you know about laying up for a neurological investigation.' He leaned forward and the room was quiet, all eyes pitying Petula and Sister Tutor, a calm woman much liked by the junior nurses, looking reproachful.

Nurse Petula Howard took a deep breath. She forced her mind back to the Women's Medical ward where she had been working on night duty for the past three weeks. Most of the investigations were done during the day when the ward hummed with activity, and white-coated doctors and students flocked to examine, prescribe and discuss the different diseases that came to the unit. At night it was rare to have to lay up trays for any examination.

During a slack period, however, the junior night sister had shown her some of the procedures and had encouraged her to lay up several trays for the use of the overworked day staff. As the one for neurological examination was not sterile, Petula had done these several times—or at least, tidied those already laid up and replaced swabs and test-tubes as necessary.

'I'm waiting, Nurse,' he said.

'I would take a tray covered with a clean dressing towel,' she began.

He snorted with derision. 'Quite a logical start, I suppose.'

The last shreds of tiredness left her as anger took their place. He was bullying her just because she was a couple of minutes late. And she'd come, even though she'd been working all night.

'I would have ready something to test each one of the senses,' she said, in a clear voice. 'A patella hammer for reflexes and a tuning-fork for hearing, cotton wool swabs for testing skin sensitivity, test-tubes of cold and warm water for reaction to heat and cold and, if necessary, sugar and salt for taste tests. Oh, yes, and a few pins to test reaction to pain. There would be an auroscope and a spatula for examination of the ears and throat, and an instrument for examining the eyes,' she added weakly, unable to remember the name of an ophthalmoscope. And I wish I could stick one of those pins in you, she thought resentfully.

For a long moment there was silence. Petula wondered if she had got it terribly wrong. Sleep had left her mind unreceptive and she was surprised that she had recalled so much.

'So you *have* been taught about it.' He was ignoring her, not praising her or admitting that she was right, except in this back-handed way. 'If this nurse knows it, why not the rest of you?'

'I work on Women's Medical,' said Petula, who had done nothing to make him better tempered. It was as if he was disappointed that she could answer well.

He turned to her. 'You have worked here for the same number of months as the rest?' She nodded. 'So it follows that they should have learned as much as you.'

'No. Some of them have been working in surgical and childrens' and ENT,' she replied.

'I see. I shall now tell you about several neurological symptoms easily recognised in specific cases.' He appeared to ignore her.

He's the kind of man who will never admit that he could possibly be wrong, thought Petula. She had the absurd impression that it gave him pleasure to see her face grow pink and her hazel eyes to gather green glints of anger. Her colour returned to normal and the rise and fall of her breast regained composure as she sank back to listen to him. His voice was very pleasant.

I must have seen him in the corridor, she thought. She'd been off sick, and missed the one lecture he gave as a stand-in for Dr O'Flyn, and this was the first time she had seen the whites of his eyes. Petula smiled. It was a fitting comparison to think of him as an enemy, ready to pounce and attack. But as far as she remembered the reaction of the class had been good after that first lecture and she had been sorry to miss it. She glanced at Dulcie's absorbed face. She had been *very* enthusiastic.

'He's a dream,' she'd said. 'He's not only

very good-looking but he has humour, too. He made jokes and we all found that we remembered what he taught us. And that, after Dr O'Flyn, is quite something!'

'Don't let one man go to your head. Just because we have dear Sister Tutor for most of the lectures, there's no need to act man-starved,' Petula had said sternly, and received a flung pillow for her rudeness. 'I haven't seen the man, so I'm entitled to think you've all gone mad to drool over him!'

'I'm not drooling. I just think I might, given the chance, that's all,' said Dulcie. 'I'm glad I came to Beatties if he's a sample of the men we shall meet here!'

And now I have met him, face to face, and neither of us seems very inclined to drool, Petula thought wryly. It's best to know the worst about him if work is going to take me into contact with him for any reason at all. Though I can't think how I've avoided bumping into him while working in Women's Medical. I expect he makes his minions do the night rounds, she decided. There was satisfaction in imagining him as unfair to others as he had been to her!

The room was warm and the chairs were a mixture of pre-formed plastic and some very deep settees that had been hastily brought over all that time ago when the first lectures had to be given in Grey Stones. It was in one of these more comfortable chairs that Petula sat now, and the voice she heard grew more and more distant.

Three months on night duty, which had
begun at a time when she was barely ready to
do such a stint, had taken much from her in
physical and mental energy. An epidemic of
glandular fever had decimated the second-
year groups and made it necessary for those
next in line to step up into more senior
positions before they were qualified to do so.

Petula yawned. Only three more nights and
she would be off for a few days—and then
she'd be sent somewhere on days again. Unless Sister Soames asked for her to stay over
the Christmas period. She smiled sleepily. Bad
luck, Sister Soames. She doesn't know that I
have Christmas leave this year, Petula mused.
It had seemed only fair to have a ballot for
holiday leave and she had been lucky.

It was quiet. It was very quiet. Somewhere
under her dreams, Petula was conscious that
the well-modulated male voice had stopped
talking. 'Nurse Howard!'

'Yes, Sister?' The room came back into
focus and Sister Tutor's face seemed larger
than life as it loomed a few inches from her
own.

'Oh!' The room seemed full of faces watching her. Dulcie had a 'don't blame me' expression on her face. Nurse Olwen Prosser
looked scandalised as usual, and Juno Maribel
had tears in her huge, dark eyes as she antici-
pated the row that must ensue. Sister Tutor
glanced back anxiously as if she hoped the
doctor had left, but he was leaning against the
table on the dais looking as if he wanted to pick

up the small nurse who had dared to fall asleep in his lecture, and drop her down the nearest man-hole.

'Perhaps our next subject should be the phenomenon of snoring,' he said icily. 'I'm sorry that my lecture was less than interesting, Nurse Howard. I suggest that you leave us and go to finish your sleep in your own quarters, while the nurses who have come here to learn, do so.'

Pale-faced and shaking, feeling the deep nausea that comes with waking in fright, Petula made for the door, leaving her books on the desk and thinking only of escape. The door appeared to be miles away and the ground seemed to rise up in flowing ridges before her, making her grab the backs of chairs and the shoulders of nurses she passed.

She swayed and Nurse Maribel jumped from her seat. Another person ran, too, and was there before the black girl could reach her friend. Petula felt her last hold on reality slip away as competent hands held her and supported her before she hit the floor.

Arms as firm as any she could recall since the time her father had hauled her out of a pond, held her with strength and surprising gentleness. Hands that could have hurt if they had grabbed her, seemed instead to gather her and soothe her into comfort.

The watch which had been given to her when she began training and which had been a family joke as it was so large for a small girl to have in her breast pocket, now dug into her as she was held fast against a hairy tweed jacket which smelled of country grasses, heather and the wide moors.

'I'm sorry, Doctor, but she wasn't really fit to come here.'

'If the girl's sick, she should be in bed.' The voice once more held a note of exasperation.

'She's just tired. She has almost finished three months' night duty and she is far too junior to do it yet. Come on, Nurse, you are all right now.' Sister Tutor sounded brisk. 'Her colour's coming back, so you can put her down again, Dr Moray. She needs to be lying flat, not caught up so that she can't breathe.'

The morning was going from bad to worse and Sister Tutor could sense that she might have to cancel her lunch date. Reluctantly, Petula opened her eyes and found herself gazing up into the vivid blue and mildly bemused eyes of the medical registrar.

'Put me down,' she whispered. The feeling of safety in his arms was giving way to something that she couldn't understand. He was holding her firmly, which might of course have accounted for the tight feeling in her breast and the sudden irregularity of her pulse, but she knew that if he didn't release her now, she would cling to him and will him to hold her close for ever. And I don't like you one tiny bit, so how can you have this effect on me, she wondered.

'I didn't know that you were so tired.' He set her down on a chair. 'It's something you'll get used to. We all have our sleep disrupted and we have to learn to cope.'

There was little sympathy in his words and he seemed glad to step out of range so that, if she had put a hand out, she could not touch him. His Scottish accent was more pronounced now and the thick hair had decided to fall in rough locks over his brow, even though he had not ruffled them.

'*You.*' He looked at Dulcic. 'Can you take her to her room?' She nodded. 'Put her to bed and don't bother to come back. There's no point in continuing the lecture—I'm sure that after this interruption nothing of what I have to say will be registered.' He looked annoyed. 'We all lose sleep at times. I could have had some rest instead of wasting my time here.'

He nodded curtly to dismiss them and turned to Sister Tutor, who was busily pushing papers into her desk, trying to get organised to go to lunch. He spoke to her in a low voice and they both looked across at Dulcie and Juno, who were walking one on either side of the drooping girl and helping her into her cloak. Sister smiled and nodded and he strode from the room, caught up his coat in the hall and opened the front door, letting a cold blast of air rush through the house.

'Is she fit to walk back?' called Sister Tutor.

'The air will do her good,' said the cruel man. He opened his umbrella and showered the last drops of rain on to the three girls before plunging out into the now clear air. He glanced up at the sky as he saw the change in the weather, furled his umbrella and held it over his shoulder like a banner before hurrying away down to Beatties.

'You forgot your brief-case!' called Sister Tutor. 'Oh, he's gone. That man leaves a trail of belongings wherever he goes.' But she was smiling, as mothers smile over the naughtiest and nicest of their children.

'Are you all right?' Dulcie held on to Petula's arm and Juno almost lifted her from the ground. 'I could ask one of the students to bring his car up here.'

'I'm fine. He was right. I needed air,' Petula muttered.

'I'd never have guessed it! I thought you'd suffocate, the way he was holding you to his manly chest. Why didn't *I* think of collapsing? How was it, being embraced by the greatest thing since waffles?' Dulcie joked.

'Don't be daft.' Petula shook herself free and her colour was normal again. 'It was like being hugged by a very hairy, smelly bear,' she lied.

'Bet it wasn't,' said Dulcie, laughing now that she had stimulated her friend to retort.

'*He* seemed to like it,' said Juno, laughing until her shoulders quaked. 'He'd never admit it, but he surely did enjoy holding you, Pet!'

'Stop teasing,' Petula protested. 'I've got the message. I'm all right now and I'm going to bed to have a long rest. But if either of you tells the entire dining-room lies about me, I'll know by this evening and you can just watch out.'

It was bad enough to have lost control and suffered the humiliation of being rescued by a man she had met only that morning but had disliked on sight. But if her friends make jokes about it and the tale was embroidered out of proportion, she would be the recipient of the kind of sniggers and rumours that grow to absurd proportions in any enclosed community.

'Depend on us,' said Dulcie.

'To do what?' said Petula morosely. 'Sorry, but I am so very tired. Bed, where are you?' They managed the stairs as the lift had stopped on the wrong floor, as usual, and while she undressed, Petula tried to sound normal again to reassure her friends. 'I shall sleep for seven whole hours and not bother with breakfast.'

'Breakfast at eight in the evening must be the end,' said Juno. She hurried away, returning with coffee and a sandwich. 'Eat this before you go to sleep or you'll feel very empty when you get up. Did you have anything to eat after you came off duty today?'

'I was far too tired.'

'You must eat.' Juno put her hands on her full hips and seemed to bloom with health and energy. 'You know the rules, girl, so why not do as they say? It makes sense. If we don't eat, we grow thin and weak.'

'And pale?' Petula smiled as the dark face split in a delighted smile. 'You are right, of course. Thanks for the coffee.' She munched happily and knew that she needed the food. 'But you know how it is—or you soon will when you go on nights. The food is the wrong way round. Breakfast when every civilised person is having supper, a peculiar mixture of food during the night, and a cooked dinner when we come off duty at eight-thirty in the morning. It makes my stomach rumble just to think about it!'

'That's hunger, not nausea. Have another sandwich. I made them before the lecture as I knew we'd be too late for a coffee-break.'

'It's nearly your lunch-time,' said Petula, amused. 'No wonder you're big and strong.'

'And fat,' said Juno with her mouth full. 'I don't care and my boyfriend likes it. You must come and have supper with us when Christmas is over.'

'I'm going away for Christmas,' said Petula. 'So is Dulcie. We drew the holiday in the ballot and you'll have to do without us for four whole days.'

'Only four? I thought you'd have New Year, too.'

'I'm grateful for small mercies. I doubt if public transport will be at its best, but my cousin said that he could fetch us if necessary.' Petula felt her anticipation growing already.

'Are you going together?' Juno was interested.

'Isn't it great? My parents are in America and there isn't a hope of seeing them, so Pet has invited me there for Christmas.' Dulcie was delighted.

'Don't expect too much. It could be rather dull. You know I live with an aunt who brought me up when my parents died. She's a dear but she lives in Tunbridge Wells and all her friends are, to put it mildly, a bit on the sober side.' Petula pulled a wry face.

'There must be places where we can go for a bit of Christmas cheer?' Dulcie asked uncertainly.

'Plenty of hotels, mostly Victorian or earlier. All red plush and silence and large bronze figures on the landings, holding torches that don't work.' She giggled. 'My aunt said she wanted to book up for lunch at an hotel, so be prepared! But there are one or two clubs where my cousin goes and the Pantiles are very picturesque and lively at times.'

'That will fill four days very well,' said Dulcie dryly. 'I don't want to carry you back here exhausted. You can't expect Dr Moray to be there to scoop you up again if you faint.'

'I suppose he had to give us the lecture now because he will be in Scotland for Hogmanay and all those other wild orgies they have across the border,' said Petula.

'I don't think so. I heard him say to Sister Tutor before the lecture that he would be here for Christmas and the New Year but had to go on a course soon after that.'

'So he'll be at Beatties, spreading his own brand of good cheer,' Petula mused. 'I wonder if he can get home from here? Unlikely, if his home is in Scotland.'

'He has a flat up the road from the hospital,' said Juno. 'When he left his brief-case, Sister gave it to one of the others to take to his home. If he has this job for a year or so, he'd have to bring his wife down here, wouldn't he?'

'His wife?'

'Most of the senior registrars are married, and he's better looking than all of the rest, so he must have a wife or a girlfriend some-where,' Juno shrugged. 'Couldn't be other-wise, could it?'

'No, I suppose not. Clear out you two, before I fall asleep again. Thanks for the food, Juno. You were right. I was hungry.' Petula promptly ushered them from the room.

She stared at the closed door and half heard the voices outside. Nurse Olwen Prosser was talking. She was easily recognised by her lilting Welsh voice and eager manner.

'Lovely flat it was. I saw right inside! Untidy though. I wanted to turn it all out and give it a good going over! He has very good taste in pictures and I couldn't quite see the photo-graphs on the piano, but one was of a very pretty girl.'

'You seem to have seen everything,' came Dulcie's cool voice.

'Oh, no! I didn't see everything. I couldn't be nosy, could I? Besides, before I could look he was back with the letters he asked me to post after I gave him the brief-case.'

Dulcie sounded sarcastic and Petula smiled, remembering her annoyance when Olwen had probed too deeply into her own affairs. 'You didn't look at the letters, of course?'

'Oh, no! I wouldn't do that! But I did just glance to see that they were stamped prop-erly. You know how it is if you get a letter and have to pay excess.' Olwen sounded very concerned.

'And were they?' Dulcie prompted.

'Oh, yes. The one to the hotel had a second class stamp and the one to his mother in Argyle was very thick and had extra stamps that should cover anything he had in there.' She paused. 'Funny to be going to a hotel in East Anglia at this time of the year.'

The voices went further away and could no longer be heard. Petula tried to sleep but now she was as wide awake as she had previously been exhausted. It was unjust! Now she had the time and the opportunity to sleep for hours and all she could do was to stare at the ceiling and think about a man she didn't want to meet again. The course he was going to do must be in East Anglia somewhere. Didn't hotels give special rates to people attending congresses out of the holiday season?

And was the letter to his mother? Mrs Moray could mean that, or it could mean that he had a wife in Argyle. Petula smiled in the darkness behind her drawn curtains. Even nosy old Olwen couldn't solve that one without asking him! He would be at Beatties for Christmas and she would be with her aunt and Dulcie in Tunbridge Wells.

She tried to think of places to visit, of people to see, and wondered why the prospect of Christmas with an aunt she loved, in a town she liked and with a friend with whom she had much in common, lacked the spark that makes for eager anticipation. David Weekes, the cousin with whom she had spent so many happy hours before they left school and went to their own careers, would be there. Dear David, she thought as she went to sleep. He might be fun for Dulcie, but that would leave her without someone. She had a sudden vision of a man with ruffled auburn hair kissing a faceless woman under the mistletoe in the medical school common-room, while carols were played softly on the record player.

Would the girl in the photograph on his piano come to warm his Christmas? Petula shivered in the warm bed. His arms would hold the woman he loved with tenderness, strength and passion. The soft curve of his mouth almost hid the undertone of firmness. Yes, there was firmness there, but there was more.

She had seen the glint of anger, which marked him as a man of arrogance. And something else, too. A relentless need to pursue whatever or whoever he wanted. So, not only was he firm but he was like a hawk, like a Scottish falcon, hovering and waiting to take his prey in his claws.

CHAPTER TWO

'WE MIGHT not be as busy as usual, Nurse, but there is still plenty to do,' said Sister Soames. She eyed the night nurse with suspicion. 'Are you sure that there is nothing wrong? Sister Tutor was quite worried about you and thought that you ought to go off sick—there's no need to be a martyr.'

Nurse Petula Howard smiled, and her pale face glowed. 'I must say that you seem much as usual, Nurse. The point I'm trying to make is that if you are on duty, you must be fit for whatever you are called on to do. If you are not fit, I would rather you said so now and I can ring down for a replacement.'

'I'm fine, Sister. I slept quite well today, at least six hours, and I ate a good breakfast.' She moved uncomfortably under the assessing glance. 'I've been small and thin for as long as I can remember, but I'm very strong. I was just very tired after a few days when I couldn't sleep, and I wasn't eating properly.'

Sister Soames clicked her tongue. 'You girls must realise how important it is to eat well when you undertake a profession as exacting and strenuous as nursing.'

'Yes, Sister,' said Petula meekly.

'Well, if you are sure you can cope, I want you to go into the balcony ward and make up

26

the beds in there. The four-bedded room used to be for infectious cases and the tuberculosis patients were nursed there for long periods when TB was one of the common diseases,' Sister Soames explained. 'Now, of course, the condition has been eradicated and such wards are no longer needed. It's been a white elephant for ages. The side wards near my office are safer to use for acute cases needing constant supervision and these beds are a bit out of the way.'

'Wasn't that risky if the patients were very ill, Sister?' Petula asked, puzzled.

'No, they were chronically ill and their progress was not usually dramatic, except in special circumstances. Their treatment was rest and good food and lots of fresh air. But that was before my time, thank goodness. We don't know the half of what they suffered, Nurse, before the sulphonamides and antibiotics were discovered.'

Sister Soames opened the glass door to the balcony and looked about her with distaste. The outer walls were made up of glass panels that could be swung back during good weather to make the ward into a sheltered balcony, but could be closed securely and warmly, as they were now, providing a light and airy room that would get any sun available.

'At least it's clean,' she said. 'They had an army of Mrs Browns in here today.'

Petula smiled. It had taken her some while to become accustomed to the names given to various types of ancillary staff. The ward cleaners were all called Mrs Brown as they wore brown overalls; the kitchen staff were known as Mrs Green, and only the porters seemed to have individual names.

Perhaps it was because they tended to stay for years at Beatties and to become a part of the fabric of the hospital, like Claud, the lodge porter, who had seen and heard so many dramatic, sad or amusing incidents that some said he could never retire in case he missed something. Olwen Prosser and Claud should have a lot in common, Petula thought.

Four bare bed-frames stood in the corners of the room and in the space left were lockers and bed-tables, drip-stands and chart holders and a viewing screen for X-rays. An oxygen cylinder on a stand had new face-pieces and its key hung by a cord round the bulbous neck of the heavy cylinder. Sister turned the key and read off the pressure. She grunted in a reluctantly satisfied way.

'I said that I would have no patients here unless we set up a small resuscitation bay. In the ward we have piped oxygen by the acute beds and everything else we might need in the clinical room, but if there was an emergency here it would mean bringing apparatus the whole length of the ward and losing valuable time if the patient was very ill.'

Petula felt slightly ashamed. Sister Soames had such a heavy load of responsibility that it was no wonder she was cross at times and couldn't afford to have nurses who didn't pull their weight. She braced her shoulders.

'What do you want me to do, Sister?' she asked confidently.

'I should be off duty, Nurse. Can I depend on you to have the beds made, the charts on the boards at the bed-ends and the rest of the things by each bed by the time Night Sister comes round at eleven? You will have to help to settle the patients in the ward until ten, but one hour should be enough.'

'Do you want any trays set, Sister?' The memory of the morning was still strong in Petula's mind.

'Yes. Can you lay up a general examination tray and the additions for neurological examination?'

'Yes, Sister.' Petula licked lips that suddenly felt dry. 'Do you know who will be in charge of the new patients, Sister? Are they separate or a part of the general ward?'

'This is the brain-child of Dr Moray,' she said, and smiled indulgently. 'He seems to think that it might be a good idea to have four patients in here, each with the same condition, treatment and food. He wants to assess them under these conditions to see how they respond in one environment. First, he wants allergy patients, hence the oxygen and the cupboard over there with a fresh supply of syringes and anti-histamine drugs. And lots of test-tubes so that the path people can take what samples they want.' She laughed. 'I grumbled at first but it makes sense. And he's such a dear that I couldn't be awkward.'

'He will be here during the day for the tests?'

Petula asked hastily.

Sister Soames looked at her curiously. 'He will do a night round as soon as we are full, but until then his house physician comes here at night. We have nothing that he need bother to examine at present.'

Petula watched Sister go to the office and then closed the door to the balcony room. She joined the other junior nurse in their haven, the sluice room, and piled warmed bedpans on to the trolley.

'Here we go,' she said, and the round began. As she rubbed the last back and smoothed the wrinkle-free sheet, she felt no relief that another round was over. Many times, friends who had nothing to do with hospital work had turned up their noses at such tasks and said that they couldn't think how she did it night after night. But the comfort and relaxation the night round brought to people who'd been lying in bed for hours at a time and at real risk of developing pressure sores, made it all worth while. Petula never pushed the trolley of soiled linen back to the sluice room without re-membering with warmth at least one or two grateful remarks made by long term patients.

'Nurse?'

'Yes, Mrs Freeman?' She knew what to expect. It was the same plea that came night after night as soon as Sister had pushed be-tween the swing-doors at the end of the ward on her way off duty.

'Could I have a hot water bottle? My feet are so cold,' the woman begged.

'I'm afraid I can't give you that, Mrs Freeman. Are you comfortable, apart from cold feet?'

'Yes, I suppose so. But if only I could have a hot bottle, a *really* hot one, just to lay by my feet, I know it would do the circulation good and I'd be able to walk better.'

'I'm sorry, Mrs Freeman.' Petula put a hand under the light blankets that were raised slightly off the bed by means of a low metal and plastic cradle. 'The electric pad is beautifully warm and it can't burn you as a bottle would.'

'Is it on? I thought you'd switched it off when you made the bed,' the woman said in surprise.

Petula gave her a drink of warm milk and the two sedative tablets that she should have taken earlier but which had somehow escaped Sister's eagle inspection.

'Go to sleep now, Mrs Freeman. You are warm and safe and you have only to call if you need someone.' She glanced at the chart, wishing that many of the medical terms had more meaning for her, but she knew about Mrs Freeman.

She had been admitted four weeks ago with a progressive nervous disorder that numbed the sense of feeling in her hands and feet and legs. While she could feel things she touched, the heat and cold sensory reflexes had stopped working, and there was a great danger that she would suffer self-inflicted burns if hot water bottles or any form of heat came into contact with the skin. The answer was to educate her into wearing thick bedsocks and mittens and to have a low-voltage heat pad for use at home.

The small burns had healed quite well and the social services were providing the necessary heat pads and socks, but Mrs Freeman was difficult to convince and Sister had doubts about her ability to cope without burning herself again. The fact that each night she still tried to persuade a junior nurse to give her a hot water bottle added to the doubts, and already there were rumblings about her going to a flat where a warden would be on call to keep her under care.

The ward was calm, and apart from the coughs and occasional snores of women who, Petula knew, would complain in the morning that they hadn't slept a wink all night, there was little sound. A lift purred in the distance and a loud voice was shushed by an even louder one along the corridor. Trolleys with ward supplies swished along empty corridors and lights went out all over the huge old hospital. There were islands of brightness as operating-theatres worked late and dim glows from acute wards and the childrens' departments. An ambulance bell stopped suddenly at the entrance to casualty but Petula hardly heard it as it had no relevance to her work in the medical ward.

As she folded a blanket to put it in the linen cupboard, and took clean sheets for the beds in the balcony ward, she wondered if anything exciting ever happened in Women's Medical. The work was heavy with so many helpless women to lift and move into different positions, and some of the treatments took time, but there was a sameness and lack of immediacy that could, over the years, become boring.

Sisters like Sister Soames were made for medical wards, Petula decided. They loved the theoretical knowledge of medical cases, which was fascinating. Or perhaps Sister Soames had fallen in love with one of the doctors or consultants on a medical firm and dedicated her life to his work!

'Quite a thought,' Petula whispered as she walked down the silent ward ready for work, the oiled trolley wheels quiet on the hard floor, and entered the balcony room.

Would anyone do that? Petula smoothed the under-blanket on the first bed and then the sheet flicked open across it with the ease and precision that had come almost unnoticed over the short months she had been at Beatties. Dr O'Flyn, who had retired as senior consultant on the medical team, must have worked with Sister for years. Many young sisters and nurses married doctors, or so she had heard, but there must be a few who had to fall in love but could have nothing of a man except the work they shared.

Petula tucked in the mitred corner vigorously. I'm being morbid. I am most unlikely to fall in love with a doctor, she told herself. I want to get my state registration, do midwifery and go to America to nurse in a luxury clinic.

She made up the second bed and pulled the

bed-table across it. The dream of success and an exciting life in America now seemed unreal. Was it the night by night routine of the ward, with few social contacts, notorious for sending most night-workers into a kind of limbo, that was dulling her pleasure in her favourite dream? America was far away and the work here was all she knew now. She made up the last bed and surveyed the room with critical eyes.

It looked neat and comfortable and with a few flowers on the desk would be rather good. So Dr Moray had some good ideas. Everyone had ignored the rather nice balcony room as unusable, but Petula reflected that if she was to be a patient, she would prefer to be nursed here than in the ward. The wall between the main ward and the balcony room was solid half way up, and then the polished wood gave way to thick, opaque glass that showed mere shadows and some filtered light through to the ward. Privacy, without being cut off from the others, was good.

She checked the trays and laid up the two that Sister had suggested. The ward was almost self-contained now as there was a small sluice, lavatory and wash-basin in a deep alcove by the fire-escape. Lights from the distant city made the sky glow and as ever, seeing the night sky of London, Petula was reminded of the great fire that had swept London hundreds of years ago.

She tried the door leading to the fire-escape and slid the bolt back. The air was cold and damp but the rain had stopped. The fire-escape had broad, shallow steps of wrought iron, a reminder of the time when buildings were made with the very best materials and beauty was not sacrificed for space. No one sees this, she thought, and yet it is well made. Her finger came away grubby from the moulding and she wiped it on a tissue. Not much clear air for TB patients if they had to sleep on a balcony above a polluted city, and it was too cold for a nosy nurse dressed in a thin cotton uniform in December. She closed the door and bolted it again.

As she switched off the lights in the room, ready to push her linen-trolley back through the ward and to ask what she should do next, Nurse Howard saw distorted figures through the glass wall. She glanced at her watch. Eleven o'clock, and Night Sister would be making her main round. The door opened and Petula put on the lights once more, glad that she had finished the job given her and pleased with the older woman's satisfied reaction. She was also very, very glad that everything was gleaming bright, the sheets tight and neat and the tables lined up with military precision, when she saw who was with Miss Tyley.

Dr Moray stood in the doorway and seemed to fill the room with an incandescent quality that came not entirely from the light through the glass wall. The room had been spartan bright before he came, but now it was his room, as the lecture room had been his and as everywhere that he sat or ate would become his for the time he occupied it. But his eyes were dull with fatigue and his hair was more untidy than she remembered it. He had spoken angrily that morning of wasting time lecturing when he could have rested . . .

Petula suddenly knew that she was not the only one who had worked hard and lost sleep. She now suspected that he had been on duty last night and had not managed to catch up on rest during the day. And here he was, at eleven at night, doing a ward round with the Night Sister.

'It looks very good, Nurse.' The woman smiled and Petula saw her glance at the doctor with concern. 'I wonder if you could make some hot chocolate for Dr Moray. He has two more calls to make and ought to have some-thing to keep him going.'

'Coffee,' he said.

'No, not coffee. Once you go from here you must sleep, and coffee will keep you awake.'

Petula waited. Miss Tyley was young to be a high-ranking nursing officer and she knew Dr Moray very well indeed.

He sighed and ran a hand through the dense hair, which did nothing to tidy it. 'All right. I'm too tired to argue, Delia.' He glanced at Petula for the first time. 'Hot chocolate, please, Nurse.' He looked again. 'Oh, it's you.' His eyes took in the details of her uni-form, her hair, which tried to escape from under the tiny cap and made falling tendrils of light golden-brown, the tight belt with the well-polished buckle, given to her by her aunt when she started nursing, and the slender legs.

'Is there anything else, Sister?' Petula wanted to run away up the ward and lock herself in the kitchen with the safe smells of hot milk, coffee and the surreptitious toast that becomes the addiction of most night nurses after weeks on duty. She was annoyed with herself for feeling like this. She had been on full ward rounds with men more senior than a senior medical registrar and not been embarrassed. She welcomed talks between consultants and Sister if she could listen and absorb some of the mass of facts and details about her patients. So why panic because one rather ungracious individual eyed her up and down as if she was a rather common variety of worm?

The milk rose in the saucepan and she turned off the gas. A pretty white mug with birds flying round the rim seemed a good choice and she poured the hot drink into it when she heard their footsteps returning. Although Sister had asked her to make the drink for Dr Moray, Petula had assumed that the attractive nurse would join him. But she didn't come further than the kitchen door.

'Make sure he drinks it, Nurse. And don't let him hang about the ward,' she added shortly. As if I could influence him, thought Petula, watching Sister Tyley's slim back recede as she went quickly away to her next ward.

'It is already sweetened, I think, but there is more sugar in the bowl,' said the night nurse, unsure if she should leave Dr Moray or not. He took the steaming mug and glanced in the saucepan. 'And there's more if you want it,' Petula added hastily. 'I made enough for Sister Tyley but she was in a hurry.'

'Then you must drink it.' Petula stepped back as if the saucepan contained poison. 'Come now, Nurse Howard, don't they teach you about waste?' A flicker of humour lit the doctor's blue eyes. 'As a true Scot, I can't have you throwing out good food—and if I drink more than this huge mugful, I shall fall asleep here.'

'I have my coffee-break later,' she said.

'I see no reason why you should enjoy fresh coffee while I have this . . . nursery muck.'

Petula poured the liquid into another mug and hoped that Staff Nurse Bolton would either come in now and be the happy recipient of a full mug of hot chocolate, or stay away until her junior had finished drinking with the medical registrar. The tin of biscuits kept on the table was obviously well known to the doctor and he sat dunking ginger-nuts in his drink while he watched the slender girl who stood so nervously in silence.

Once, she stole a glance at her watch, but it was difficult to do so unobserved. He asked what the time was, although he had a gold wrist-watch in full view. Petula blushed, knowing that he had noticed her attempt to see the time without him thinking that she wanted him to go.

'It's as big as Big Ben,' he said. 'I wondered what massive object was digging into me this morning.' She blushed still more deeply. When she had changed her clothes the round bruise left by the pressure of the watch showed clearly how closely he had held her in his arms when she fainted. 'Remind me to show you the bruise,' he said with a wicked grin. Instinctively, she put her hand over her watch-pocket. 'You too? You should see a doctor.'

'If you've finished, I'll take the mug,' Petula said stiffly. 'And Sister Tyley was anxious for you to get to bed.'

'Yes, Nurse.' She turned away, acutely aware of the blue eyes regarding her back. 'But I have to stay for a while. I asked my house physician to meet me here to learn the details of what I want in the end ward tomorrow.' He frowned. 'Come on, Ros. Come on!'

He sat back in the chair and closed his eyes. Petula had an irresistible desire to giggle and he opened one eye and smiled. For one lovely moment, there was a bond of shared humour and warmth as if they were old friends. He had seen the link between the tired nurse who couldn't keep awake and his own condition.

'I think someone is coming now,' she said, and her heart was still beating fast when the door opened to admit Dr Rosalie Arran, the beautiful doctor who made the heads of patients and staff turn to her as sunflowers to the sun.

'About time,' he said, but the curve of his mouth relaxed into a tender smile. 'Come on, Ros, I'm dead on my feet. Let's see the room and you can get down to it tomorrow.

Dr Arran nodded to the night nurse and stuffed her elegant hands into the deep pockets of her white coat, making the mundane garment look as if it had come from a fashion show. Softly, they walked through the ward, pausing to glance at a clipboard here and there before disappearing into the end room.

The light shone softly golden through the thick glass and cast no harsh light or shadow across the sleeping faces in the ward. Petula washed the cups and put some coffee to filter for Nurse Bolton. Suddenly the bleeper in the pocket of Dr Moray's coat made her start. She picked it up, as guilty as if she was picking his pocket, and was glad that she knew how to turn it off before telephoning to answer the alert.

'This is Sister Tyley. Has he gone to bed yet?' Petula explained that Dr Moray was with the house physician and wondered why Miss Tyley was so cross.

'I would like to speak to him on the internal telephone *now*, before you ring off, Nurse.'

Petula put the phone down and left the bleeper on the desk. The light was still on in the small ward as she went swiftly and silently down to the door. It opened without sound and the two people looked up at her.

'A call for Dr Moray from Sister Tyley,' she said. Rosalie Arran brushed her dark hair back from her flushed face and pushed the doctor gently away from her. He let his hands slide from her waist and slipped past the small nurse without a backward glance. The house physician stood up and took a deep breath.

'You can put the light out now, Nurse.' She went into the ward and picked up each clipboard in turn, making a note here and there and taking her time, as if she wanted Dr Moray to leave the ward before she did.

Petula switched off the lights. As the room plunged into darkness, with only the distant lights of the city in the sky, she knew that a tiny flame that had struggled to live when she had been with Dr Moray in the kitchen had been snuffed and killed before it had a chance to show its rainbow colours.

The office was empty when she returned and Petula switched up the heat under the filtered coffee as Nurse Bolton pulled back the curtains from the bed of the patient she had been treating. Dr Arran came with her and glanced first at the empty chair and then at the night nurse, who stared at her and didn't smile.

Petula poured coffee for the two women and wondered how the doctor could speak so normally only a few minutes after she had been surprised in the end ward. Surely she must know that Nurse Howard had seen her held closely in Angus Moray's arms, her head on his shoulder and his face close to hers?

'How is Mrs Freeman?' asked the doctor, as cool and professional as if nothing untoward had happened. Or perhaps it was nothing unusual. At night, there must be many quiet corners where a man and a woman could snatch a few minutes of heavy petting, or at least the odd kiss and caress.

'I haven't seen her tonight. You did her bed with Sister, didn't you, Nurse Howard? And you saw that she took her sleeping pills?'

'Yes, Nurse Bolton. I'm afraid that she still asks for a hot water bottle as soon as Sister is out of the way. Can they send her home like that?'

It was easy to discuss patients and to ignore what her heart was telling her. The attractive woman who spent many hours with the medical registrar had plenty of time and opportunity to make him fall in love with her. She was good at her work, which must make a great contribution to anyone as efficient as Dr Moray, and she was beautiful. Could any man with red blood in his veins work with such a woman and resist the desire to take her in his arms when they found themselves alone?

'Goodnight,' the doctor said at last. 'I have to be here early tomorrow to get the cases installed. They'll all come in with their skin tests done and we'll begin investigating their food allergies, starting at lunch-time. Dr Moray believes that if patients know the worst about their conditions and how they can be helped, they will have fewer psychological attacks through fear. They can carry medicaments and have instructions on Medicaire medallions so that they can be helped at once if an attack threatens. He's a great comfort,' she said, and the smile on her lips as she walked away was not for the two nurses but for some inner memory in which they had no place.

'That man!' said Nurse Bolton. 'He'll forget

his head one day.' She held up the bleeper, which had been lying on the desk.

'He might have left it on purpose as he isn't on duty now. I heard him tell Dr Arran that she would have to cope with the note-taking and first treatments tomorrow,' said Nurse Howard.

'You don't know him as I do. He leaves things all over the place. If there's a spare stethoscope lying about you can be sure it's his, and the times that Sister has bleeped him to collect brief-cases, X-ray pictures and white coats are too numerous to mention!'

She frowned. 'He ought to have this, though, in case he is wanted in a hurry. Now, I can't send you out of hospital in uniform if you are to come back on the ward again in the same clothes, and anyway, it wouldn't be a good idea to be wandering about this district at two in the morning, so we shall have to leave it until the day staff come on. While I'm giving report to Sister, you could nip up the hill to his flat and hand it in.'

'But I don't know where he lives, Nurse.' Petula protested.

'You don't?' she sounded very surprised. 'I thought that most of the staff here had flowed through his flat at one time or another, for one thing or another,' she added, with infuriating vagueness.

Did she mean that he had a steady stream of women visiting him? Was this man with the bright hair and sapphire blue eyes a lecher? Someone had said that a man like him must have a wife or a girlfriend tucked away. And what if he had a wife to whom he wrote long letters in far-away Scotland *and* had many girls in his flat in London?

'Have you been there, Nurse?' Petula asked casually.

'Oh, yes. I went there a lot last spring soon after he came here.' She chuckled. 'I was probably the first here to go with him in that camper-van. Very cosy and very comfortable.'

Petula found her face stiffening. 'Then, wouldn't it be better if you took this?'

'Oh, no. We gave each other all we had to offer ages ago and I have other interests now.' Nurse Bolton shook her head. 'No wonder he gets tired. All those late nights after the birds can't be good for a man with a job as exacting as this.'

The night seemed endless and most of the petty jobs that Nurse Bolton found for Petula were done long before the morning rush of treatments was due to begin. It was a relief to be busy again and to have people with whom she could talk and help to greet the day fairly cheerfully. How could he? Petula asked herself for the hundredth time. How could a man with those honest blue eyes be such a creep? It was almost impossible to believe, but she had seen him with Dr Arran, holding her close. And who knows what would have happened if they had been alone for much longer?

'Make some tea before the day staff come, Nurse Howard. We've time for a quick cup.' Petula poured boiling water over the tea-leaves and filled the mugs. She handed the one that Dr Moray had used to Nurse Bolton, hating to handle anything he had touched, and yet wanting to possess and to cherish anything that was his.

'Here for Christmas?' said Nurse Bolton, as if it was a foregone conclusion.

'I drew a lucky card. I'm going to my aunt in Tunbridge Wells.'

'Staying for New Year?'

'No. That's rather a pity. She belongs to a good group who do highland dancing and they make a great party of Hogmanay.'

'Do you dance?' Nurse Bolton looked at the slim figure and the trim ankles and thought Petula would look good in the tartan. In fact, if Petula dressed well, she could be pretty. 'Well, you can dance here. We have our own talent.' She smiled and hurriedly went to answer the bell of her patient in the side ward.

'Who dances here?' called Petula, but she couldn't hear the reply, and soon the first of the day staff appeared.

'Nurse Howard!' called the staff nurse from the side ward. 'Take that bleeper over to Dr Moray now. I've put a thermos of coffee on the desk. I'm sure he can use it. Tell him I'll have the flask back tomorrow and not to forget it.'

Blankly, Petula looked at the bright orange vacuum flask and the small bleeper that she had to take to the doctor. 'I'll tell Sister that you have gone and explain why. Go off duty and have a good meal. You look pale again.' Nurse Bolton put the dirty syringe into a waste-bin and made a note that she needed more adrenalin for injection.

'Thank you, Nurse,' said Petula unhappily, and put the bleeper in the pocket of her dress. Carrying the large flask before her like a bright orange light that might, if she was lucky, protect her from evil, she made her way out of the main building and breathed the early freshness of the morning.

Somewhere a bird tried out a few notes as the sun decided that today it was London's turn for a bit of cheering up. The pavement was dry and Dr Moray's flat in a tall Victorian building half-way up the hill was easily found. Petula wished that it was half a mile away in an unmarked block, which would have given her the chance to go back and say she couldn't find it. But there it was, his name, efficiently written in very black capitals on a neat card by the door. Dr Angus Moray MD FRCP.

Angus? He really is Scottish, she thought. Her heartbeat quickened as she pushed on the outer door and it gave before her hand. With any luck there would be a table outside the flat on which she could put the bleeper and the flask, so that she could ring the doorbell and run away. She giggled.

The flat was on the next floor and she tiptoed up the tiled stairs to the small landing. There was a table, but it was covered with a peculiar collection of articles that included a badly worn duffle coat, a white hospital coat that looked as if it had been used under a car, a small haversack and a very expensive camera.

Petula gasped. How careless! Anyone could walk in and take that camera without being seen.

She stood there trying to find the courage to tap on the door. If he left valuables at risk, she couldn't follow his example. Her finger was hovering over the bell when the door was flung open and she was nearly knocked over by a tall blond man she recognised as Dr Lou Sheridan, the casualty officer of Beatties. He grinned and looked at her legs. Then he saw the flask and his grin turned to laughter. He looked back inside the flat and called, 'Visitor to see you, complete with breakfast. You can't get them to stay the night so you have them bring you coffee in the morning! Lucky for some!'

He seemed to think he had made a very funny joke and was still laughing when he picked up the worn duffle and the camera and ran down the stairs. Petula hovered in the doorway until a voice told her to come in and shut the door, or get out.

She walked in slowly and closed the door gently. Her voice wouldn't obey her. Twice she tried to call that she was leaving his bleeper on the table in the sitting-room, but she could make no sound come. Water from a shower stopped abruptly and Dr Moray came into the room with just a towel round his waist and his hair dripping over his eyes. He groped for another towel from a pile that included other clean laundry. Instinctively, Petula reached across and took a large towel, which she thrust into his hand so that he wouldn't drip water all over the clean washing. 'Here,' she said.

He rubbed his face and pushed the hair from his eyes. 'Thanks.' He stared and the blood under his skin gave away his astonishment. 'Hell! Not you again?' The fact that he shared her embarrassment as they recalled the situation in which she found him the night before, did nothing to diminish her own distress.

'I brought your bleeper,' she said, and it sounded inane.

'You brought my bleeper.' He stared at her.

'And Nurse Bolton insisted on sending this for you—and can she have her flask back?'

'I bet you were the one they sent to get the football when it went over into the glasshouse.' He smiled and she found her own lips twitching. 'Thank you, Nurse Howard, but for once, I did know where I left my property. I had no intention of being called out of bed for at least six hours.'

'I know the feeling,' she said.

'The kitchen is in there.' He waved the towel in the general direction and vanished into his bedroom, emerging one minute later with faded jeans zipped tightly over his hips. Droplets of water still lay on his shoulders and over his breast was a dull blue shadow that matched the one on her own. Such an intimate sharing that would never be revealed.

He took the flask which she had placed on the draining-board and poured the coffee into two mugs.

'Cheers,' he said, and she lowered her eyelids before the intense and now sombre gaze. 'I'm sorry,' he said. 'I had no idea that you had been on night duty when you passed out during the lecture. It was my fault for trying to fit in one lecture to relieve the pressure of work in the New Year.' He shrugged and the wet shoulders glistened under the light.

'You weren't to know,' she said.

'As you weren't to know that I was tired, too.' He handed her the towel. 'Dry my back. I can never reach without doing a contortionist act.' She breathed deeply and began to rub his shoulders, trying to imagine that he was a patient. But it was difficult to think of him as anything but a man who filled her heart and mind. She dried him with smooth, even strokes that gave away nothing of her feelings.

'Now my hair.' It was a command, and her hands trembled. His hair was thick and cold now that it was drying and she rubbed it vigorously until the brightness began to show. 'Do you know anything about Addison's disease?' he asked.

'No.' Petula picked up a strand of hair that was dry at the ends. Thank goodness he was talking shop.

'I was up all night with a patient and he died on us.' His disbelief and shame were mixed. 'We did all the right things, but he died.' He took the towel from her hand and flung it away, drawing her with him into the sitting-room and down beside him on the settee.

Petula's eyes were hazel as a spring wood, flecked with young green, and her mouth was pale and vulnerable without lipstick. Tiny painful breaths shook her as he bent to kiss her and she wanted to give him comfort, love and all that he asked. She opened her eyes as his mouth left hers and glimpsed the photograph that Olwen had seen. It was on the table behind him and was of a very lovely girl whom she recognised as Sister Delia Tyley. She was standing by a motor camper and was dressed in a pair of brief shorts and a sun top.

Petula pulled away from Angus Moray as his mouth descended on hers again. Longing for him fought with her growing repugnance for a man who, to her knowledge, took women with him in a kind of mobile love-nest, who thought junior nurses were good for coffee and sympathy and made love to female medical staff in darkened rooms.

'I came to give you back your bleeper,' she said, and fled, only stopping running when she got into the warm, comfortable dining-room among others of her set. And the worst memory was of his amused laughter following her as she ran.

CHAPTER THREE

'OF COURSE we do far more important work in Casualty than you do on the wards,' said Olwen Prosser with a smug expression on her pink face.

'You reckon?' said Juno mildly. 'I find I have quite enough to do on skins to keep me busy. Some of the treatments seem to go on for hours.'

'Oh, well, skins are something special. You get a lot of personal responsibility there, too. Dressings are far more interesting than the boring old round of bedpans and backs and water-jugs.'

Petula finished her coffee and went to get more from the pot on the table. It was a rare occurrence for her to meet any of her set during their off duty time before she went to the ward, and she had hoped that she would be able to talk to Juno Maribel for half an hour. But Olwen had come to join them in the sitting-room of the nurses' hostel and threatened to take over.

What is she getting at? Petula wondered. Olwen seemed to be trying to goad her into making some kind of rude retort. There was nothing specific, just a niggling jibe or two to make her feel that she was, as night nurse on Women's Medical, in a humble and menial position.

'Medical isn't all bedpans,' she said firmly. 'We have very good ward reports from Sister Soames and the more I hear, the more I know I have to learn. She knows as much as some of the senior doctors and has a way of putting it over that makes it all seem simple. I envy her.'

'You wouldn't like to stay there for ever, like Sister?' Olwen looked shocked. 'I can imagine nothing worse. I don't think you meet many interesting people there.'

'I never thought I would like it, but I find that I shall be sorry to leave. If I can go back there on day duty, I shall be very pleased,' Petula insisted, calmly.

Olwen laughed and looked knowing. 'Of course, you do have Dr Moray there, don't you?'

'He is the senior medical registrar,' said Petula.

'Are you jealous, Olwen?' Juno laughed, trying to take the edge from the conversation. She glanced at the set face of the night nurse and wondered if she was perhaps a bit too up-tight.

'Jealous? When I have that lovely man, Dr Sheridan, on Casualty?'

'He does seem very friendly,' said Juno. 'I met him when I fetched a patient for admission from one of the clinics and he was very helpful and amusing.'

Olwen looked slightly sour. It was good to boast of the rapport she had established between herself and the handsome Canadian doctor, but she didn't want to hear that he used his charm on everyone. 'He's very polite, even to people he doesn't really know,' she said, 'but when you get to know him as I do, then you see the real man.'

'I think we're all lucky,' said Juno soothingly. 'We have some great guys here, and if I didn't have my boy-friend, I'd fall for all of them.' She laughed, and the deep musical sound made Petula smile too, but Olwen looked annoyed.

'Dr Sheridan tells me all sorts of things about people here. He knows all the consultants and the registrars and most of the sisters. I could tell you a lot if I was indiscreet,' she added, as if wild horses wouldn't drag confidences from her.

When neither of her friends reacted with gasps of surprise and curiosity, she reddened. 'He told me about you and Dr Moray, for a start,' she said, giving Petula a triumph look.

'Me and Dr Moray?' The blank face convinced Juno that Olwen was making mischief yet again, and she got up as if bored and poured more coffee.

'It's true.' Olwen watched Juno come back and stir sugar into the hot liquid. 'He told me that Nurse Howard was seen going into Dr Moray's flat up the road very early this morning. Too early for her to have been off duty, and she was taking him his breakfast.' Olwen looked from one face to the other. 'I didn't know that the hospital supplied thermos flasks for the use of nurses, Petula. That's what he said you were carrying. He said that Dr Moray wasn't even up and dressed when you went there.'

'He also told you that Dr Moray was in the shower, and I went in and shut the door?'

'Well, yes.' Olwen looked less confident and her eyes lost some of their spite. Petula remembered that it was Olwen who had been to his flat to take his brief-case and that she hated anyone to catch up with her. In another week, the visit to his flat would have taken on a certain hush-hush quality, as if Olwen had been invited there personally.

'So it *is* true,' she said, triumphantly.

'Quite true,' said Petula, icily. She smiled in such a way that Olwen knew she had said too much. 'In fact, I can tell Juno and anyone else interested that the flat was exactly as you said it was, even to the photograph of the girl by the camper-van and the general untidyness. So that makes two of us who have been in his flat so far, and if he leaves any more of his belongings about the hospital I think that, in time, most of our set will be very familiar with the place.'

She saw that Olwen was wavering. 'I had to take his bleeper to him. He left it on the ward during the night. He hadn't slept for at least thirty-six hours and Nurse Bolton sent him some coffee. Satisfied? If you want to know more about him, ask her. She has been out with him in that passion-waggon and so have some more of the staff of Beatties, so if he invites you, you will be one of a crowd. Stick to your nice gossipy friend, Dr Sheridan, Olwen! He sounds as if he would put up with anyone, even you.'

Petula ran to her room, the tears very close to the surface, and flung herself on her bed, furious with Olwen, furious with Dr Sheridan and even more furious with herself for rising to the bait. Olwen seemed to rub everyone up the wrong way sooner or later. What did it matter that she made snide remarks about Dr Angus Moray? It wasn't important that a man with hardly a stitch on had made a pass at her!

But under the turmoil of her anger, she knew that what hurt the most was the fact that she had responded to his kiss. She had wanted his body close to hers and the painful imprint of that ridiculous watch bruising her breast and making its mark on him so that he must remember her! He could smile if he must, but he'd remember her.

At least now she was fully awake and the adrenalin was flowing again. She looked up syringo-myelia in a textbook and knew that she could answer questions when Sister Soames wanted to know what she had found out about Mrs Freeman.

The allergy cases might be interesting, too. David, her cousin, the man with whom she had been brought up under the roof of her generous Aunt Merriol, had hay fever each year and dreaded the fine, dry weather when all his friends enjoyed the grass and the hot breezes.

Perhaps Dr Moray will discover a marvellous cure for it, Petula thought, and shook herself for dreaming. Was it impossible to think of a subject as serious as an allergy without making that man a part of it? It was becoming increasingly difficult to find any subject in which she didn't see him, with his richly red hair and the kind of blue eyes that froze or reduced her to jelly.

She put her watch in the top pocket of her dress, a couple of ball-point pens and a small notebook in her other pocket, and patted her hip to make sure that it was not too bulky. Her cloak was on the chair and she looked back to the cosy room and wished that she could go out with Juno and Dulcie this evening instead of spending the night on a ward where the possibility of Dr Moray appearing was very disturbing.

She walked down to the lodge to fetch the evening paper that Claud kept for Sister Soames and to buy stamps from his inexhaustible supply. He greeted her from the tiny wooden cubby-hole he ruled and occupied from morning to night, unless he had to go on an errand of importance, like seeing what kind of cases came in by ambulance.

'You're on Medical, aren't you, Nurse?' Petula nodded, amazed that the man in the lodge should know where every nurse worked and most of their private affairs, even after such a brief time at the hospital. 'Take this up, will you? It's for Dr Moray. He'll be doing a round tonight, I expect. You have four admissions up there today.'

She smiled. How could he know that?

'My friend in Casualty told me about the balcony ward. As if you haven't enough to do, Nurse!' His raised eyebrows invited grumbles which would be passed on magnified, as Petula had heard.

'I really came for Sister Soames' paper,' she said. 'And some stamps, Claud, if you can spare them.'

He bent to pick up the battered biscuit tin in which he kept stamps, rubber bands and odd change for telephone calls. 'Anything for me?' she said casually, not expecting anyone to send her letters to the main building.

'One from Tunbridge Wells,' he said. 'Looks like a brochure or a large programme.' He squinted at the hidden illustration under the semi-transparent wrapping. 'Not going to sunny Tunbridge for the summer are you, Nurse?'

'No, I'm going for Christmas,' she said, and smiled. He doesn't believe me, she thought. Why is it that certain towns like Tunbridge Wells and Chipping Sodbury make people smile and treat them as figments of the imagination?

'That's a laugh, isn't it, Doctor? Nurse says she's going to Tunbridge Wells for Christmas.'

Petula turned to see Dr Sheridan grinning behind her. 'Why not, Claud? Some of my best friends come from Tunbridge Wells.'

Their laughter followed Petula and she

knew that Dr Sheridan was regarding her with more than a little interest. He couldn't really think that she had gone to the flat by invitation, could he? In any case, he was less than her favourite person after telling Olwen about her.

She went to the ward, aware that she was early. She lingered in the corridor but it was too obvious that she was killing time there, so Petula went on to the ward and put her cloak in the duty room shared by all the staff. It was even used for talks between consultants and students if Sister was busy in the office and they wanted to discuss patients in privacy.

She slipped the shiny plastic cover from the package and saw that it was from her aunt. Knowing Aunt Merriol, she wasn't surprised that she had forgotten the address of the hostel and had sent it to the main hospital block. Petula flicked the pages over and read a few dates and events that were to happen over the Christmas holiday, the local Caledonian club being mentioned often. The Hogmanay celebrations would be very good and there was a picture of one of the leading hotels showing a previous meeting, with a large crowd of guests dressed in tartan and enjoying a really Scottish evening.

There wasn't time to read it all and she left it on the table, pinned down by her notebook to make sure that it wasn't taken by someone thinking it just a circular meant for anyone interested. Sister Soames was in the office.

'Reporting for night duty, Sister,' she said.

'Nice and early,' said Sister, cheerfully. 'I have time to give you report on the new cases that came in today. Dr Arran has been very busy all day. I have never seen her work so hard. Already we have the first skin patch tests in the path lab for early charting and we started everyone on a bland diet at lunch-time. We'll introduce various foods gradually as the days go by and watch for reactions. Do you understand why, Nurse?

'At home, we are never sure if patients do exactly as we ask. It must be very difficult if you are the mother of children and you find a half-eaten bar of chocolate which you eat, although you suspect that it makes you feel ill. Most people eat made-up dishes and fast food things that might contain small amounts of substances which upset them, and if they aren't eaten in isolation, they never really believe us when we tell them to avoid them.'

'Does it work in reverse, Sister?' Sister Soames looked pleased at Petula's quick question.

'You've been reading about it? You are right to a certain extent. There have been patients who come to us with the firm idea that they dare not eat certain foods because their grannies told them they were bad for them, or some such nonsense. It takes a while to get them to try such foods and to know that they can eat them. For example, the eggs in fruit cake might upset them, so they think they can't take dried fruit either, when they might like it in other ways.'

'What do I do first, Sister? Is Nurse Bolton here yet?'

'She's talking to Dr Arran. See to the water-jugs and then nurse will be ready for bed tidying and the bedpan round. One of the admissions, Mrs Livingstone, came in after lunch, which was a bit naughty as we asked them all to be here earlier. She isn't very well, so I hope she isn't bringing in gastric flu or any other form of gastro-enteritis. She made the excuse that she had just come back from visiting her son and that some food had not agreed with her there.'

'Is she in the balcony room, Sister?'

'Yes, we don't think it is an infection and she had a history of bad allergies, so it might be one just appearing. She was very hazy about what she ate and none of the others in the family show any signs of being upset, so we assume that this is her usual problem.'

Sister frowned. 'However, Nurse, we must take all possible care, and until we get results of faecal tests she must have her own set of crockery. Be very careful to keep a labelled bedpan for her, making sure it is disinfected after use. I needn't stress the need for thorough hand-washing.'

Petula nodded. Sister told her a few further details and looked up as she heard footsteps outside the office.

'Are you nearly done, Dr Arran?' Petula stepped back into the room. It was Angus

Moray. The voice she dreaded sent shivers of something other than dislike over her and her hands were cold.

'I think that's the lot for now Angus, but I would like you to look at Mrs Livingstone. Sister knows the score and I think it's an allergic reaction. She has a slight rash and some urticaria,' came Rosalie Arran's voice from just outside.

Sister Soames went into the ward and Petula felt trapped in the office with the two doctors standing by the half-closed door.

'I'll see her now,' said Dr Moray. There was a pause and a sigh. 'Now, I thought we had agreed, Ros? Just because you panicked last night, there is no need to work yourself into the ground to make me know that you are dedicated to your profession.'

Petula thought she heard a sob.

'Come on, now. I didn't beat you, did I, just because you misread my intentions? We all make mistakes. It was just a misunderstanding! You *will* come to Norwich with me, as we arranged?'

'You don't hate me?'

'Ros, how can you say that?' Petula imagined rather than heard the light kiss he planted on the dark hair and the footsteps went away, allowing the student nurse to escape.

He was trying to persuade Dr Rosalie Arran that his bold approach in what he thought was the privacy of the empty ward was not the humiliation that Rosalie must have felt it to be!

In all fairness, Petula thought, she must have felt as I did when Olwen hinted that there was something between Dr Moray and me. Was that his usual ploy? Did he make a woman sorry for him and then lead her on to love-making?

He had said that a patient had died and had released that flood of remorse that made Petula a ready target. Had he used the same tactics with his house physician? And she had panicked when she saw the night nurse watching the embrace.

It should be quite easy now to look on him as a very competent doctor but a scheming swine as far as women were concerned. And Norwich? That was the place where he was going to a hotel out of season. If Rosalie got cold feet and wouldn't go, it would upset his lovely, illicit weekend, Petula thought grimly.

The clank of bedpans was satisfying. It would have been even more satisfying if Petula had been able to throw them from a great height, preferably on one auburn-haired man who aroused such tumult in her heart. Briskly, she gave out her bulky load and made sure that all the cubicle curtains were drawn tightly. She tidied the sluice room and began the second round to collect the pans and to make the patients comfortable for the night. The other night nurse helped for a while, but she was seconded to the men's side as they were very busy, and Nurse Bolton took over when beds were to be straightened.

'Have a good sleep?' she asked, and Petula

relaxed. Nurse Bolton was so cheerful and matter of fact that it was difficult to feel annoyed. They set up a rhythm of back rubbing and powdering with the variously scented talcs that the individual women produced as soon as they saw the hospital issue.

'What is it tonight, Mrs Ross?' Nurse Bolton sniffed as if smelling some exotic dish. 'Ah! Gardenia!' Mrs Ross looked pleased and they settled her thin legs comfortably, noting that she had more colour after her second transfusion.

'I'm feeling ever so much better, Nurse. Dr Moray says that I can go home next week after I've had one more lot of blood.' She looked at Nurse Bolton as if she was indeed a healing angel. 'You've all been so good to me. I never thought I'd have the strength to go out of here alive. I'll go out feet first, I told my husband.'

'Nice for him,' murmured Nurse Bolton. 'Poor man, he looked petrified when he saw the blood drip, but he knows now that she will be quite well if she comes in for her regular tests and transfusions for pernicious anaemia.'

'Does she have any drugs, Nurse?' Petula asked.

'She will have injections of B12, one of the B group vitamins, in the form of cyanocobalamin to replace what she has lost and can't make for herself any more. All her symptoms of breathlessness and weakness and general debility will be much better,' said

Nurse Bolton as soon as they were out of the patient's hearing. 'It was the lack of ability to absorb vitamin B12 that gave her the condition, but if she has it by injection, either in the clinic or from the district nurse, she will have a better life than she dreamed was possible.'

'That sort of thing makes up for a lot, doesn't it?' Petula smiled. Even Nurse Bolton had fallen for the charm of Dr Moray and now boasted that she was one of the first to go with him in the camper-van. And yet she was serene, as if she had never been in love. In time, Petula promised, in time, I shall laugh at the memory of this week and lose myself in satisfying work and the gratitude of people like Mrs Ross and Mrs Freeman, who was at last coming to terms with her disability.

The light from the end ward was still on after the main ward was quiet. Nurse Bolton looked uneasy.

'Can you finish the end two beds? They can shift their own bottoms for you, as they get up during the day. I ought to go to Sister. She should have been off ages ago. I hope nothing is wrong.'

Petula tidied the last bed and dimmed the lamp over Mrs Ross, who had begged to be allowed her light until the beds were finished as she wanted to finish the last chapter of her romantic novel.

'I shan't sleep until I know it's all right,' she said, and when Petula went to turn off the light she was smiling happily.

'I take it they live happily ever after?' Petula enquired lightly.

Mrs Ross smiled even more. 'I do love a happy ending,' she said, and closed her eyes for sleep.

The ward was neat and quiet, and yet there was a feeling of tension coming from the end room. Sister could be seen bending over one of the beds, her shadow against the glass wall, and now Nurse Bolton was in there too, leaving Petula to cope with the main ward. She walked slowly to the end by the balcony room, sensing that she might have to fetch something or to take a message. She glanced at the clock at the end of the ward and saw that Sister should have gone off duty at least an hour ago. She had mentioned a dinner, but she would never get there now. Something must be wrong.

The door opened and Sister Soames came out, 'Bleep the house physician, or better still get Dr Moray. And hurry, Nurse, tell him he's needed urgently.'

With trembling hands, Petula tried to alert the doctors. But there was no reply and she tried to ring the common room. Suddenly, she heard the door at the end of the corridor swing as someone came out of the men's section. She bleeped again, and this time the call was answered by the voice that was becoming as familiar to her as her own. In seconds Dr Moray was in the ward, dragging on his white coat as he came.

'You just caught me,' he said. 'I came in

from a meal and thought I'd check on one of
the men.' He looked at her anxious face.
'What is it?'

'Someone in the end ward, Dr Moray. Sister
said it was urgent.' He sped down through the
ward like a silent wind, and Petula hurried
after him, unsure what she must do. If only she
was more experienced and could anticipate
what they might need, instead of standing
helpless, mentally frustrated by her desire to
be of use!

The door opened. 'Nurse Howard?' Sister
seized her arm and took her into the room so
that other patients could not hear what she was
saying or see what was happening.

'Find Dr Arran and tell her to bring a set of
tracheotomy tubes at once. We may not need
them but there is a possibility. Then lay up a
tray for the operation. You have it in your
notes?'

'Yes, Sister.' Petula cast one frightened look
at the woman on the bed and ran as fast as she
could, not caring if the patients saw her. What
had they said in PTS? Nurses never run except
for fire or haemorrhage! This was neither, but
she was running as if her own life depended on
it, as she suspected the life of the woman in the
bed depended on swift and skilful care.

She had the picture etched on her mind as
she ran. Mrs Livingstone, the new admission,
was lying helpless and nearly unconscious, her
face a peculiar mass of swollen tissue and her
eyes like lost currants in a suet pudding, as if
she had been inflated by a balloon-pump. She

was gasping for breath and even a nurse with Petula's lack of experience could see that something drastic must be done soon.

Dr Arran answered at once and gasped when she heard what was needed. 'Angioneurotic oedema?' she asked.

'She is very swollen and can't breathe,' said Petula, unsure of herself.

'Laryngeal oedema,' said Dr Arran and put down the telephone. Just as the tray was laid, Petula heard footsteps running towards the door. So even doctors ran sometimes, even when it wasn't a cardiac arrest!

In the first lectures they had been shown tracheotomy sets and all the students had taken it for granted that they were never used now that diseases like diphtheria had been conquered. Sister Tutor had been quite annoyed, saying that if they ever had to see one done, it was something they would never forget. She went on to tell them that in accidents or in some kind of blockage to the air passages, the operation was life-saving. And all that rainy afternoon, she had made them lay up trolleys and trays for such emergencies.

Now, Petula blessed her for it and was confident that she had the right dressings and the other things necessary. She had a small steriliser boiling to receive the tubes, but the ones that the doctor brought with her had been autoclaved in a steel drum and were ready for use.

Dr Arran thrust the box into the nurse's hands and hurried after her down the length of

the ward. She was carrying a syringe in a sterile
dish and had a few glass phials in a box. As they
opened the door, Petula could hardly refrain
from crying aloud. Mrs Livingstone was much
worse and her colour was very bad indeed.
Sister Soames took sterile instrument forceps
from a bowl of disinfectant and transferred the
sets on to the tray, glancing with approval at
Petula as if to say that she had done well. Dr
Arran was busily filling a syringe with the fluid
from a large phial. The sombre face Dr Moray
lightened.

'Good girl,' he said. 'We tried the other and
it made little difference.'

'You think it might work?' He nodded and
wiped an area of the bloated skin with a spirit
swab before the rubber cuff was inflated round
the swollen arm and Dr Arran put in the
needle to find a vein.

Petula watched, fascinated and horrified.
How could anyone find a vein in that mass?
Angus Moray was tense but a pulse-beat
in his temple was his only sign of anxiety.
At the third attempt, blood came back
into the syringe and everyone gave a sigh of
relief. Dr Arran looked up into the blue
eyes.

'300 milligrams of hydrocortisone sodium
succinate. Check?' Dr Moray nodded and the
fluid level in the syringe went slowly and carefully down.

Sister Soames cut a piece of oiled nylon
which would go on top of the dressing for the
tracheotomy if it was done. She obviously

didn't believe that whatever they gave would work.

How can it work? thought Petula, but the man with the steady gaze seemed to emanate confidence and trust and something that Petula wished was directed to her and not to his lovely colleague. Did something of his confidence flow through the syringe and into the veins of the sick woman? Whatever happened, the result was staggering. The woman on the bed gasped, took the first deep breath she had taken for too long, and her colour began to improve.

As if by magic, the drug took effect. It fought the reaction that had made her body release fluid into the tissues, as if responding to a thousand insect bites. Petula had seen men and women swollen after bee and wasp stings and allergic reaction to some foods, but this was frightening until the effect was reversed and the shock reduced.

Sister Soames put the oiled nylon back in the packet and came to the bedside. She saw the look of wonder and disbelief on the face of the nurse and smiled.

'Panic over, Nurse,' said Dr Moray. 'Thanks to Dr Arran, she'll do. All we have to find out now is what caused this attack, and I think that we might know more when her family visit her.'

Sister looked at her watch. 'I think I might arrive at the dinner in time for some dessert and coffee,' she said, but she didn't sound as if it was important. 'Clear the tray, Nurse, I doubt if it will be needed after all.'

Mrs Livingstone was still very swollen, for the oedema in her tissues would take time to absorb, but she was conscious and able to co-operate and had lost the terrible rasping effort to breathe.

Petula carried the tray back to the clinical room and stripped it. She then went back to gather the used syringe and broken phials and the soiled swabs used for the injection. Nurse Bolton was taking the pulse rate of the patient on a new chart, having already recorded her respiration rate and general condition. Even the measurement of her arms above wrists and elbows was recorded to show how much the swelling reduced from hour to hour. The face-mask of the oxygen apparatus was changed and the night nurse took it to the clinical room for cleaning before placing it back with others of varying sizes by the cylinders.

It was a wonderful feeling to be a part of the team concerned with saving the life of Mrs Livingstone. I did nothing really, Petula thought, but there was a warm sense of belonging to the ward, to the system and to the Princess Beatrice Hospital.

Only one small part of her being was cold and empty. Dr Angus Moray had given her no word, no glance. She could have been a fly on the wall as far as he was concerned. He had eyes for Dr Arran alone, and his gaze followed her with an almost protective tenderness that Petula ached to be hers.

At last the patient was comfortable and an

assistant nurse was sent up from Casualty to sit
with her while the staff of the ward went back
to the routine work. By the time that she was
told to go down for her meal, Petula was very
hungry and had the false brightness of night
duty workers once the first wave of tiredness
has gone. She went into the duty room for her
cloak and to fetch the local magazine that she
had received from her aunt, and saw that
someone had been looking at it. It was open at
a page advertising the Caledonian Club meet-
ings and the reference to the Hogmanay
celebrations.

Slipping it into her pocket, Petula felt for
her watch and remembered that she had left it
on the desk in Sister's office. It was much too
big for use on duty and twice she had nearly
lost it down the sluice when she had bent over
to rinse some towels. Only its thin chain saved
it, and she knew that often the chain was loose
if she was in too much of a hurry to fix it
securely. I'll have to get a small watch that pins
on, like Dulcie's, she thought. The wide sweep
of the second hand had made her choose it, but
it was like a watch that men wore on watch-
chains years ago and not really suitable for a
small nurse with few pockets in which it would
sit safely.

Petula picked up the papers and her notebook and tapped on the office door. She heard
the murmur of voices and thought that Nurse
Bolton was there. She pushed on the door and
heard Dr Moray say, 'Does this make up for
last night? I told you that you wouldn't run out

on me a second time . . .'

Petula decided that her watch could wait until the doctors had left and she stepped back quietly, unseen, to go to the dining-room.

CHAPTER FOUR

'I'M AFRAID I had no alternative.' The senior nursing officer sounded faintly on guard and wondered why Nurse Howard was so silent. 'You did have Christmas away from the hospital, Nurse, and you know the ward well. It will only be for a few nights and this time the tests are for gastric acidity and should have no moments of drama.'

She smiled encouragingly. Perhaps Nurse Howard, who was, after all, much too junior for night duty and far too inexperienced to see such alarming cases as the angio-neurotic oedema that had blown up in Women's Med just before she left for Christmas leave, was scared of what she might see if she had to go back on the same ward for a few more nights.

'I understand, Miss Bright,' said Petula. 'You want me to report tonight?'

'I wouldn't ask you to do this extra night duty on Women's Med if we had our full complement of staff, but the glandular fever has taken at least seven nurses and they will be away for several weeks. The two new nurses cannot come until the new year and the surgical units are slacker than usual—no one likes to be in hospital for operations over the holiday season.'

'I like the ward and I should like to go back,' said Petula politely, hoping that the thudding of her heart was not perceptible to the keen-faced woman who looked at her so uneasily. But it was a shock that must have shown in her eyes and in the tense muscles of her face.

'Well, that's settled, then.' Miss Bright's relief was evident. 'Go to bed now, if you think you can sleep, and report on duty at the usual time. I can offer you an extra day's leave when you come off and go to surgical in the new year, and if you have the time, I shall tell Sister Tyley to let you rest for an hour after your midnight meal.'

So, it was back to the balcony ward and back to the medical firm of which Dr Angus Moray was the medical registrar. Petula had been so sure that, once back at Beatties, she was unlikely to see him again in a working situation. The odd meeting in the corridor and at social functions would be bearable, but now her sense of safety was shattered. Tonight, she knew, he would be there, walking the ward and demanding attention. To make matters worse, Dr Lou Sheridan had promised to find her for a chat wherever she worked and to make final arrangements about the Hogmanay dance.

Christmas at the home of her aunt in Tunbridge Wells had been warm and full of laughter, good food and the gentle feeling of belonging to a long tradition of reverent celebration. For most of the time Petula had lost herself in the soft cloud of tradition and memories. But twice she had seen the festival as something passing away from her—as if she might not see it again in the same way. As she had gazed deep into the embers of the log fire on Christmas night, unwilling to think of returning to London, the flames had seemed to lick the sides of the fire-back as if to destroy and not just to warm . . . Dulcie had been free of such dark thoughts and Petula knew that she was already half in love with David, Petula's cousin. Was it a sense of envy that cast this cloud over the brightness? Was she jealous of her cousin and her best friend?

Perhaps I sensed that I was to go back to the balcony ward, she thought, and smiled as she left the office to go back to her room and unpack.

And the New Year party? Would she be off duty for that? It was one way of avoiding the man who knew so many women and seemed to love them all a little, yet always looked round for more easy conquests. Sister Tyley and Dr Arran would be more than enough to fill his time at any party. He wouldn't notice the absence of one small girl with slight hips and dainty feet.

'What did she want?' Dulcie came into Petula's room, carrying the soiled clothes destined for the washing-machine in the utility room.

'I'm back on nights.' Dulcie groaned. 'Only for a night or so and she was very nice about it,' Petula went on.

'So I should think! We aren't even due for

night duty for a while and you seem to live on Med! I suppose it *is* back to Med?'

'I do know the ward,' said Petula. 'It wouldn't be worth breaking in a fresh nurse for three nights.'

'You sound as if you are a tight shoe!'

'I feel like one that has been stretched too far,' said Petula with an attempt at humour. 'I'm not looking forward to Dr Amorous Angus. Not that it affects me,' she added hastily. 'But I shall have to learn to knock on doors and wait until I'm invited in if I want to save myself embarrassment.'

'I don't get it!' Dulcie sat on the bed and frowned. Mellowed by spiced wine after the wonderful dinner on Christmas Day, Petula had told Dulcie what she had seen and heard in the ward and in the flat where Dr Moray lived. 'I know he sounds as if he is a roué but he just doesn't seem like that. Usually my skin crawls when someone with that sort of a reputation comes within yards of me, but he has everything it takes. He's kind and good with patients, the students respect him and the nurses drool after him. Even the ones who find fault with doctors in general give him credit for sheer niceness,' Petula had puzzled.

'I only know what I saw and heard. I don't want to believe it, although . . .'

'Although you fancy him?' Dulcie speculated.

'Of course not,' said Petula crossly, the hot blood flooding her cheeks. 'I have every admiration for him as a doctor, that's all.'

'Did you have a good Christmas?' Juno Maribel put her head round the door and beamed.

'Great!' said Dulcie. 'How did things go here?'

'Wonderful. The surgeons and senior doctors really went out of their way to help and came in to carve turkeys and to give out presents. I had a lovely parcel from home and my boyfriend managed to get down here for Boxing Day.' Juno laughed. 'It was so easy with the wards thinned out, and we had only two men who were very ill—and even they perked up for the day.'

'One of them was the bad chest from men's med, the one who is for theatre, I suppose?'

'He's having bronchoscopy soon, but he is much better now that he's in a warm and constant atmosphere. He tried to tell the doctor that his condition wasn't due to being out of doors in all weathers, but she wouldn't believe him.' Juno laughed. 'But she seemed to know all about it! I can't imagine Dr Arran living rough, can you? She told him that it was possible to be out for long periods in bad weather if proper meals were eaten and that the periods of exposure were linked by periods in warm surroundings with plenty of rest.'

'Do you like her?' said Petula.

'Sweet woman,' said Juno, warmly. 'And so upset about the Addisonian crisis who died. She took all the blame for his dying and that nice Dr Moray had to shake some sense into her. He'd told her what to do while she waited for him but she didn't give the patient a big enough dose of the drug.'

'Then it was her fault,' said Petula. 'Anyone with a conscience would blame herself.'

'No, she couldn't know. The man came in for checks after being in a road accident. He was shocked but not wounded and he carried no sign that he was having to take steroids for Addison's disease. They didn't know what was wrong and, to give her her due, she was the one who guessed what might be the problem. They asked him and he said he did have to take drugs but didn't remember the name.'

'So what happened?' Petula asked curiously.

'They say that if someone is on steroids of that kind, and they are withdrawn, especially with the patient in shock, they are very ill unless the dose is given and increased.'

'You *have* learned a lot,' said Dulcie, with genuine admiration.

'I love the evening reports,' said Juno. 'I get so interested that I read textbooks in bed!'

She laughed, and Petula once more envied her lighthearted enjoyment of life. It was impossible to be with Juno for more than half an hour without reluctant smiles teasing the corners of her mouth as warmth and friendliness washed over her tired spirit.

'Anything exciting happen? Like Olwen running off with someone, for good?' said Dulcie mischievously.

'Olwen isn't so bad,' Juno said. 'She does care about her work. When *she* sends someone up to the ward from Casualty, they have all their notes and X-rays, which is more than can be said for the Junior Staff Nurse there.'

'She gets up my nose,' said Dulcie coarsely. 'I suppose she was sucking up to the men all through Christmas?'

Juno shook with laughter. 'You guessed it! She happened to stand under every sprig of mistletoe in Beatties and must have been more than satisfied with the response.'

'Did she manage to get Dr Moray?' Dulcie glanced at Petula, who pretended her belt was twisted and had to look away.

'No, he was busy most of the time, but he did come to the Boxing Day party with Sister Tyley. He brought a big van into the car park by the medical school and everyone was dying to look inside. Sister Tyley helped him load a lot of packages in it. Enough tinned food for a safari, and waterproofs. Do you think they are going to elope?'

Petula recalled the picture of the attractive night sister standing by the camper-van clad in brief shorts and a revealing sun top. What a busy man Angus Moray must be, she thought wryly. One woman helping him to pack for a trip somewhere, and another agreeing to go to a hotel in Norwich soon after Christmas. Very clever to make it in a hospital where everyone gossiped and knew of an incident before it happened! Did Sister Tyley know about Dr Arran and the other women who openly said that they had been with him in that luxurious van?

'I saw Dr Sheridan,' said Juno. 'We missed him over the holiday.' She looked serious. 'Olwen heard that he had gone to Tunbridge Wells for Christmas and knew that you had gone there, too. I'm afraid she was very cross and began to hint that you were running after him.'

'That girl will be for the chop soon, if she doesn't cool it,' said Dulcie. 'I hope to goodness that she didn't see him driving us back to Beatties!'

'Oh, no,' Petula shrugged. 'Ah, well, can't be helped. *We* know that we only saw him at a party and he had dinner with my cousin and some friends.'

'Which included you, of course?' Juno smiled.

'Fraid so. It turned out that his friend in Tunbridge Wells was none other than David's friend, Andy, so we all spent quite a lot of time together. David and Andy are coming up for the dance.'

'And Lou will tell Olwen.' Dulcie's face was miserable.

'What does it matter?' We know what happened. Why should a nasty-minded girl affect us? Just because she fancies Dr Sheridan it doesn't mean that everyone in the hospital must keep away. He doesn't belong to her.'

Dulcie looked very upset. 'If your cousin comes here and Olwen reads into our relationship more than exists, I swear I shall hit her! I refuse to be embarrassed by her.'

'Calm down,' said Juno. 'We can deal with

her when anything like that occurs. 'Who is this cousin, anyway?'

'He's just a very sweet man who took pity on me and taught me how to dance Scottish dances.' But Dulcie was pink-cheeked and her eyes grew soft as she talked of David.

'Well, if I am to get a couple of hours rest before I eat my second breakfast of the day, will you please get out of my room?' said Petula. 'I can't think that I shall sleep but I might drowse if I try to study the signs and symptoms of bronchitis.'

'Better look up gastritis if the patients in Women's Med are in for tests.' Juno took out a medical book and handed it to her. 'My boyfriend gave me this for Christmas.'

'How romantic,' said Dulcie, smiling. 'He must think you very beautiful.'

'I would have been more flattered to be given flowers or candy,' said Juno, 'but he did show sense.'

Petula glanced through the textbook and became interested, although the subject matter was far too involved for such a junior nurse to understand without more experience. Juno was engaged to a pathologist in another hospital who wanted her to be a qualified nurse when they married and returned home to Ghana. It must be very important to him to help her, Petula thought as she tried to feel tired enough to doze away the afternoon and early evening.

Sleep evaded her, but she knew she wouldn't feel very tired on the first night of this shift. A false brightness would take over, making everything very clear-cut, as if she had taken stimulating drugs to get her through the difficult hours when the hospital became a strange place of soft noises and empty corridors, sad dreams and the triumph of recovery.

I must prepare myself to meet Dr Arran and Sister Tyley. I must be able to do my work as if they had no relationship with Angus Moray, the man who seems to have this great power over women, Petula decided, wondering if Dr Moray would make love to the pretty night sister in the cosy confines of the camper-van. Would she lay her head on that firm, broad chest and listen to his heart beat out his love for her? Petula knew she could melt in that situation.

She slid out of bed, annoyed with herself and utterly unable to lie there without thinking of him. He was a flame that seemed to be extinguished, only to flicker and burn in unexpected places when she thought that she was safe. I don't like him. I despise him for what he is, she tried to believe, but she knew that the thick hair lay heavily on his brow and the deep-set eyes held strength and power and would darken with desire if he found the one he could love for ever.

'And that isn't you, so stop being a fool,' she said as she dressed once more in uniform and made sure that she had everything she would need for the night. She looked for her watch and then remembered that Olwen had told her that Lou Sheridan had taken it from Dr

Moray's flat. Petula bit her lip. She had forgotten it in the flurry of Christmas away from the hospital, and she wished that she had mentioned it to Lou when they'd met in Tunbridge Wells.

'Damn,' she said softly. All it needed was for Olwen to simper up to Lou and tell him that the watch belonged to Nurse Howard. Lou's attitude towards her had changed during the break and she now knew that he viewed Olwen's gossip with reservation. Now, though, it could start up again . . . more tiny vicious flames singeing her pride and reputation. Surely he would believe what had happened—that she had left the watch in the office and Angus Moray had picked it up absent-mindedly, as he did so many things?

The Christmas tree in the window of one of the sitting-rooms looked tawdry through the dusty window, even though the light was bright behind it. So soon after the holiday, yet it looked used, as if it needed to be dismantled and the decorations put away for another year. Nurse Bolton caught up with Petula on the way to 'breakfast'. She was smiling.

Petula looked at her, trying to see beyond the smile. If she had been one of the doctor's conquests, how could she seem so unconcerned, so happy? Was it only the Christmas decorations that were dead? Was there anything more dead than a brief affair, a flame that burned and left no warm ashes? So many people lived like that, loving and giving in to fierce desire one day, and turning from it to light a nonchalant cigarette the next. I couldn't, she thought.

'Is the ward busy?' she asked Nurse Bolton.

'Not too busy, but we need staff for the end room. We have to do four-hourly aspirations of stomach juices and put them in carefully labelled pots for the path lab, tomorrow.' She laughed. 'Don't look so fraught! It's easy and you just do as it says on each chart. You don't have to pass tubes or anything ambitious like that. All *that* has been done and the equipment is there by each bed.'

'If they have tubes, are they allowed up for toilet purposes, Nurse?' Petula tried not to sound too worried.

'Oh, yes. They have small rubber tubes strapped to their cheeks, with tiny spiggots blocking the tube ends. They can talk and swallow quite normally once the tube is down and the other end in the stomach. There's a small weight on the end of each tube to keep it *in situ*—I'll show you a Ryle's tube when we get on duty and you'll see what I mean.'

I never thought I'd want to hear about stomach tubes as light relief from my more morbid thoughts! But at least I know that work is going to save my sanity, Petula decided. 'Sounds interesting, Nurse Bolton. How many women have we in there?' she asked.

'Four when I went off duty last night. There had been some talk of two more and there were two spare mattresses taking up a lot of room.'

'Is there room for more than four? Not very nice for the patients and very cramped for bed-making, I would have thought.'

'Exactly. Sister had a word with Dr Moray about it and I wonder what was said. He does get the bit between his teeth at times. Bags of exhausting energy, that man.'

'And you should know!' said Petula. 'I mean, you know more about him than I do,' she finished more diplomatically.

'Yes, that's the nice part of working in the same hospital for several years. I think I know him very well, and not only as a doctor.'

Petula sensed the genuine affection in Nurse Bolton's voice. Affection but nothing more. His touch did nothing to generate affection or a gentle friendship in Petula. She touched her apron over the breast where the dark bruise had faded. His impact was deep and forceful, with a threat that endangered logical thought.

'You look hungry. Come and eat, even if you don't feel like it. It's a long hard night,' said Nurse Bolton kindly. 'You might have time to rest for a bit after midnight. When Sister is out of the way you could kip in the duty room for an hour.'

'Miss Bright suggested that,' said Petula.

'Well, that makes it official! You can rest without worrying if Night Sister will find out.' Nurse Bolton talked until they reached the ward, telling about the various celebrations and the amusing things the children in the unit had said and done when a famous disc jockey had come in as Father Christmas before his breakfast show on Christmas morning.

'You know,' she said, 'It's often the ones you least expect to have the time or committ- ment who come and do these wonderful things for hospitals. I wonder if he got more satisfac- tion out of the children here than out of his own family scene?'

'Funny men are often very serious people,' agreed Petula. And so-called serious people can hide rather unpleasant tendencies under a smooth surface, she thought.

'Ah, there you are, Nurse. I was telling Dr Moray that you would be coming back to us for a while.' Sister Soames smiled. 'At least you know where everything lives—and we should be able to manage without you in a night or so.' Her manner was vaguely apologetic, as if she knew that she was asking a lot of a nurse who was really too junior to do the work allotted to her. Dr Angus Moray stared as if he had never seen the slender and now slightly pink young nurse who stood in the doorway looking as if she feared he might pounce on her at any moment.

Nurse Bolton hovered in the background. 'Good-evening, Sister. Do you want me for anything or shall I check with the day staff?'

'Wait a moment, Nurse.' Sister Soames pursed her lips and the doctor looked annoyed. 'There has been quite a lot of re- organising,' said Sister. 'Dr Moray is in a great hurry and wants more patients admitted than we can cope with at this moment.'

'I just need two patients as controls, Sister,' he said coldly.

'But not in the balcony room,' said Sister firmly. 'I know they are ambulant, but it would be impossible for the nurses to make beds with six in there.'

'If all the nurses are as slim as Nurse Howard, they can manage just fine,' he said, and Petula tried to ignore the glint in the devastating blue eyes.

'I know you want this batch to be done before you go away, Dr Moray, but you must remember that the balcony beds are extra to my normal numbers and make for a lot of extra work at a time when we are short staffed.' Sister was not going to be easily defeated.

Petula hid her eyes under her thick, long lashes and hoped that Angus Moray didn't see the glimmer of a smile on her lips. He looked so cross and his eyes glowed with suppressed arrogance. His brows came together like a dark line of thunder and she was glad that this time, at least, she was not the cause of his displeasure. Full marks to Sister Soames for keeping at least some of the reins of authority in her own grasp.

Dr Moray stood tall and gazed down to the end of the ward across the many empty beds. 'You don't appear to be overworked, Sister,' he said shortly. 'I'll settle for two patients to be admitted into this ward. In fact, I would prefer it—the controls should ideally be away from the ones on test.' He smiled with heart-tearing sweetness and Sister smiled, too.

'That's different,' she said, 'so long as they need no treatment. We may have empty beds until after New Year, but I really can't spare nurses for extra patients.'

'They will give no trouble, I assure you, Sister.' Petula glanced up and saw that the doctor was watching her. His eyes now sparkled with wicked humour and with a shock she knew that he had got exactly what he wanted from Sister Soames but was leaving her with the conviction that she had given not a single inch in her resolution.

'Don't just stand there, Nurse,' she said briskly. 'We need fresh aspiration trays. Clear the used ones completely and start afresh. It's good practice for you and if you do them as well as you did the tracheotomy sets that, thankfully, we didn't use, then you will do well.'

Nurse Howard blushed and hoped that Angus Moray would believe that she was blushing with pleasure at the unexpected praise, though in fact it was because she had to brush past him to get to the ward and her skirt conducted a strange and sensual impact from his white coat, as if he was charged with a force that could excite or destroy. Petula took a deep and slightly shuddering breath and tried to walk away calmly.

The empty beds lay starkly white under the soft night-lights and most of the patients were at the near end of the ward, close to Sister's office, the clinical room and the duty rooms. Cubicle curtains were round two of the beds but this was for toilet purposes and none of the patients was dangerously ill. The far end of the ward was shadowy in a gloom of twilight, with light from the balcony room glowing through the semi-opaque walls of frosted glass. It was like a ship anchored outside a harbour, tied to it, but leading a separate existence, slightly remote.

Nurse Bolton was looking at charts. 'He could have used the ward for the tests,' said Petula.

'No, it does make sense,' said Nurse Bolton. 'He wants as little contact with normal patients as possible. You know how it is in a general ward. Someone offers a sweet, regardless of the fact that it might be forbidden, relatives bring in horrendously unsuitable food that gets passed on to other patients . . . We can't monitor everything brought in. In the end ward, we can vet each visitor and make sure that the patients eat and drink nothing forbidden.'

They reached the balcony ward and Petula heard footsteps behind them. She opened the door and went in, sensing that someone came after her. She pretended not to notice this and took the first of the aspiration trays to clear in the tiny sluice bay. She turned to fetch the second one and found Angus Moray examining a chart by one of the beds. Petula bit her lip. She knew that she should take the tray from the locker near to him, but she made a detour to the one at the far end. She cleared that tray and knew that she must now go to the one she had missed. The doctor turned as she approached, and held up a chart.

'You know what you are doing, Nurse?' he said.

'I'm doing the trays, as Sister asked me,' she said.

'But I hope you know what the treatment will be?' He stood by a bed that, although taken by a patient, was at the moment empty. It was unlikely that the other patients could hear his voice clearly.

'I haven't had report yet and I'm only just back from Tunbridge Wells.' Petula looked down at the tray and tried not to think how stupid it sounded, almost like the first time she had spoken to him after the disastrous encounter in the lecture room. Why had it to be Tunbridge Wells?

His lips twitched. 'I see! I suppose it is unreasonable to imagine you learning anything there, except Scottish dancing.'

'How did you know?' For a moment ordinary female curiosity overcame the crisply dressed nurse who tried so hard to be professional whenever this prickly-mannered man came into view.

'I expect it is common knowledge by now. If you don't want your activities noted you should be more careful with whom you spend your weekends and holidays.'

'Is it newsworthy to spend time with an aunt I see all too infrequently?' Lou Sheridan must have said something. Yet in Tunbridge, he had seemed to change into a friend, not the type of person who tried to chat up any girl he met.

His genuine interest in Scottish dancing had been touching and she recalled his boyish enthusiasm when he met the members of the Caledonian Society at the practice dance on Christmas Eve. He had played the bagpipes to ear-shattering effect and had also drunk a fair share of Scottish drams. At the time, Petula had decided that he was a lonely man, far from his relatives in Canada at a time when it was good to be with nearest and dearest.

As they had walked back to her aunt's house, the air had been clear and frosty with the magical sense of something waiting in the wings. He had tried to kiss her when they were in the shadows of the Pantiles and she had pushed him away, but she had raised her face to receive a goodnight kiss when he kissed each of the women farewell.

He had talked about Beatties and the friends he had made there. It was a sharp pleasure to hear about Angus Moray and his work with allergies, but the sharpness dulled when Lou laughed as if he had a secret about Moray that he wasn't telling. He hinted that Sister Delia Tyley might be involved and that Rosalie Arran was a great friend of the clever doctor. It was hard for Petula to keep up a facade of polite interest even though her heart sank in despair. And now it seemed that Lou had been gossiping to Dr Moray, making something out of nothing.

'I asked if you knew what we had to do? Am I so terrifying that you retreat into coma each time I speak to you?'

Petula started. Dr Moray's mere presence had an overwhelming influence on her and probably on other women. 'I was waiting for you to tell me, Dr Moray.'

'This batch of patients are women who suffer from some form of gastritis. The one thing they have in common is over-acidity, and we want to see if this condition improves with various anti-acid preparations, with rest in bed or with treatment for stress. Three patients have red stickers on the charts, which means they are on full diet. That is, they eat a carefully measured amount of various well-balanced foods and drinks. They drink only what we provide and each one has a different substance put down the Ryle's tube to combat any acidity. The two who will be in the general ward are controls and will have the same diet but no medication while the tests are in progress. In fact, they are normal people who volunteered for this test, accepting a rest in hospital for a few days while they have minor treatments for other conditions that needed dressings but no drugs.' He looked at her expectantly.

'You said you had four patients and that three have red stickers. Is the last one a control, too?' she asked quickly.

'In a way. We wanted to note the effect of smoking on gastritis. We know it has an effect on the heart and here we are testing its influence on the stomach. We may find an interesting answer when we cut down Mrs

Bence's smoking during the final stages of the test.'

He smiled as he talked and Petula knew that his work was his love and his life. All other considerations like the love of a woman would take second place. His eyes held the glow of an evangelist and she wanted to be taken into his fold of converts. But it will be only into his professional fold, she thought, and smiled sadly at the irony. She saw the slightly gaunt and determined jaw and the glittering eyes and knew that this was no shepherd, but rather the wolf who despoils the flock. It would be no protection, being in his fold, professional or not . . .

Sister Bolton put her head round the door and smiled. 'Are you ready for report, Nurse?' She looked at the used tray and her face hardened. 'Really, Nurse Howard. I sent you to do the trays and you haven't even collected them yet!'

'Please don't blame Nurse Howard,' said the incredibly smooth voice with the fascinating caress in its Scottish undertone. 'I was explaining about the latest batch of cases and I'm afraid I detained her.' Petula stared. Dr Moray was actually making excuses for her! 'She doesn't seem to know a great deal about gastrics, Sister, so I was trying to fill in the gaps that an efficient sister tutor could do as routine for first year nurses.'

He picked up his folder of notes. His blue eyes held a steely triumph. That round to Dr Moray!

Sister tightened the muscles of her face and ignored him. 'Carry on, Nurse. I want you to go round with Staff Nurse as soon as you have finished here. We may not have many beds in use but we need all the help we can get to make sure that the patients don't suffer because you have your time wasted in idle chat.' She stalked away and Dr Moray put back his head and laughed.

Petula hoped that her back was ramrod straight as she walked away with the tray. In the tiny sluice, she sighed.

'Ever felt like a football being kicked between two people?' she asked the tired-looking plastic dish before she tossed it into the waste-bin. Dr Moray had no time for her, either as a sensible woman or an efficient nurse. She attacked the tray with disinfectant and put a clean cloth to cover it, repeating the process with each batch and adding the dishes, aspiration syringes, swabs, spare towels and the covered jugs needed. A separate tray was set with spare Ryle's tubes, the fine tubing with weights at the distal end to make sure the tube went into the stomach and rested there safely. Petula carried the trays back and left them neatly covered on the bed-tables.

The smell of tobacco smoke greeted her and Petula saw a large woman strolling back from the main ward with a cigarette in her lips. 'Mrs Bence?' The woman smiled and coughed. 'I think you should stay in here if you are smoking. Sister told me that you were only allowed to smoke in the bay with the extractor fan working.' Petula touched the switch and the noiseless fan cleared the air.

'I saw her,' said Mrs Bence, 'I'm back now, aren't I?'

'Fine. I'll be back shortly to tuck you all in!' said Nurse Howard, smiling. She could imagine Sister in fine form, telling Mrs Bence what to do, for she had already been ruffled by the handsome doctor who seemed to have things his own way wherever he went.

Petula looked back at the small ward. Light, distilled through the outer glass walls, came from the distant city skyline and made a late sunset. Sounds, muted by the breeze, which took the harshness away, had a cosy familiarity. Nothing seemed to intrude on the peace of this little ward. It was a good idea to have the allergy tests done where the patients could relax away from the general rattle of bedpans and the voices of staff and other patients.

The four women sat up in bed with the thin tubes strapped to their faces, talking against a background of music from a small radio on one of the tables. The atmosphere was warm and relaxed and Nurse Petula Howard had a sudden flood of almost sentimental pride in the neat room and the row of gleaming specimen bottles, all labelled ready for the next aspirated fluid. She checked what she had put on the trays and remembered that there was not enough sticking-plaster for four more changes.

She had to walk past Dr Moray, who seemed to be spending a long time in the big ward, and when she came back the second time he appeared to watch her walk the whole length of what now seemed at least a hundred yards of bare floor. To Petula's relief, Nurse Bolton came out of the office to meet her.

'Everything all right?' she called to the doctor. 'Nurse Howard, shall we tidy beds and settle them in the end bit? We can aspirate now and then the next sample will be taken at five am.' She turned to check something in the office.

Petula stopped and waited for the staff nurse to join her. She heard the low-voiced exchange as Bolton passed the doctor and wondered if they were laughing at her. Bolton was smiling as they went together into the balcony ward.

'He's a gem,' she said, but didn't elaborate, and when Petula muttered about rough diamonds she only looked amused, as if she had far more glowing jewels in mind. 'Everybody comfy?' Nurse Bolton asked cheerfully.

'Nice change, Nurse,' said Mrs Oxford, chewing reflectively on her Ryle's tube. 'They won't find nothing out from this. My tummy is nicely settled in here with me being waited on. If they give me a tube when I'm in the supermarket, they might see a different picture!' She settled back on the pillows and sighed. 'But I'm not grumbling. Got sick leave, haven't I? Got everything done for me and no worries. My two kids are giving hell to my husband's mum, which makes me feel great. Even he looked worried when he saw the tube in!'

'Make the most of it,' said Nurse Bolton. She looked at her watch and, once again, Petula missed having a watch of her own to consult. 'Before you go for a break, Nurse, could you sort out the box in the duty room? Sister wanted it done tonight and she hates the Christmas leftovers. Some wards keep their decorations but she likes them all down before New Year. It's a pity in a way, but it also makes sense. If we get a sudden influx of patients after Christmas we shall have no time for clearing up paper and holly!'

'Yes, Nurse.' Petula looked back at the silent ward. If Dr Moray was to come back now, he would think there was nothing that needed even one nurse on duty. And if he caught her turning out decorations, he might even be justified in his opinion. She cleared a space on the big oak table that was used for note-making, a resting-place for spare aprons and lecture notes and a favourite seat for doctors with time on their hands and a pretty nurse to talk to during the hours of the late night round.

The box was large but light, and she heaved it up to the table and saw the tangle of paper and plastic inside. She turned it all out in a heap on the table and picked out the more obvious rubbish destined for the incinerator. A paper angel, only slightly bent, looked sad and she reluctantly added it to the rubbish. Next year it would look even more sad and be discarded, so it might as well go now.

'Goodbye, little angel,' she said, and found

another in slightly better shape. She looked at it from all sides.

'Throw it out,' said a deep voice. 'Shabby angels have no place here.' Petula swung round, the angel in her hand, and saw Dr Angus Moray leaning against the wall, regarding her with faintly sardonic humour. She went pink and put the angel in the rubbish bin. 'Only the pure and holy come within this hallowed room,' he said, and she knew that he was being as sarcastic as possible. He came towards her and sat on the edge of the table with his hands behind him. 'Don't let me stop this serious task,' he said. 'Sister will be very cross if you don't obey her instructions, however idiotic they may be.'

'I am only a junior nurse, Dr Moray. I do as I am told and try to take . . . insults if I have to do so.'

She rummaged in the heap, hoping that he would go and give some other hapless being some of his rudeness, but she knew that he was still there. The room seemed filled with a light and brittle tension that could only be the emanation of some strong emotion. On her side, it was anger, or she desperately wanted to think it might be. On his side, it was dislike of such depth that it was threatening. It had to be, didn't it?

Petula held up a handful of paper streamers and then some bright baubles that looked like blobs of coloured candy. She refused to look up and when she next held up her hand, paper streamers dripped from it, but in her fingers she found a sprig of artificial mistletoe.

'The luck of the dip,' he said softly. 'I'm glad I was here.' He took the sprig from her nerveless fingers and seemed to loom above her, the shadow of the stupid plastic spray making a pattern on her face. Powerless to move, she saw his mouth descend on hers as the firm lips met her trembling softness. She knew that this was being suspended in time. This was the icing on the cake and the angel at the top of the tree and she wanted it all, the icing and the cake and everything that made this devil so sweet.

'No,' she said softly, but her body refused to obey her instinct to run away. He gathered her into an embrace that sapped her will and her power of reason. He kissed her again and the plastic spray fell to the floor.

'Well, well,' he said, as he released her. 'Now I know what Lou was hinting at when he told me that you had given him a Christmas kiss.'

Petula put cold hands to her hot face and watched him go. The tatty remnants of the decorations seemed sordid and used, and she wanted to join them among the rubbish.

CHAPTER FIVE

'YOU LOOK better than you did a few nights ago,' said Sister Soames. 'A few nights did I say? It was before Christmas that you had your traumatic experience and the man died, wasn't it?'

Rosalie Arran sighed. 'It was a nightmare, Sister. I did all the wrong things, or thought I did, until Angus made me see sense and pull myself together. I accept now that I couldn't have saved him, but I'm getting a fixation about patients on steroids carrying a card or some form of identification disc everywhere they go.' She smiled. 'But I feel all right now, and after a peaceful weekend away from London everything will be resolved.'

Nurse Petula Howard busied herself with the pile of X-rays that Sister wanted sorted out before the night round, and it looked as if Dr Rosalie Arran was the one who would do that round. Petula had dreaded coming on duty but she knew that if Dr Arran did the round, she would be able to act normally.

She shuddered as she thought of the incidents of her last night on duty. After Angus Moray had left her among the tattered remnants of the Christmas decorations in the duty room, she had tried to still the shaking of her hands and the wild beating of her heart. What could have been fun, a kiss from a very handsome man under a piece of mistletoe, had left a feeling of sadness and angry frustration. It was so obvious that he had been told something about her by Dr Lou Sheridan. But why? Why should Lou cancel out his fresh and more realistic opinion of her and revert to thinking that she was just another girl who could be pursued with no regard for convention or for her reputation?

Petula's shoulders sagged as she recalled what had followed. Lou had come into the room minutes after Angus Moray left, smiling as if he was confident of a warm welcome.

'I saw Moray leaving,' he said. He leaned against the table and his smile was calculated. 'Quite the English gentleman—or do they have them in Scotland, too?'

'What do you mean?' Petula asked.

'Once more, I dangled a certain watch before his eyes and he just stared at it as if it was an adder.' Lou took her watch from his pocket and swung it to and fro as if doing a music-hall act involving showy hypnosis. 'I was told that this belonged to you.' Petula nodded. 'I *was* surprised. Everything that Nurse Prosser hinted seems to have more truth than I thought.'

'I told her where I left it.' Petula put out a hand, hoping that he would stop the stupid teasing, but he held the watch high and laughed.

'Nurse Prosser said you left it in his flat when you went back—for something she didn't specify, but which I can guess.'

'Lou, please give me back my watch. Olwen Prosser is a spiteful bitch and if you believe her, you'll believe anyone.' The gleam in Petula's eyes was the residual emotion left from her encounter with Angus Moray, but Lou thought it was exciting and attractive, and for him. There was more to the small nurse with the wide eyes and soft hair than he could have hoped.

'Come on, now,' he said softly. 'You have to pay me for it.' He held it towards her. 'Come and get it.'

'Lou, you've got this all wrong! I told you I'd left it on the desk in the office and you know how Dr Moray leaves bits lying about and picks up things with his notes. He's famous for it in the hospital. He probably didn't notice until he was back in his flat and then forgot to give it to me.'

'So he did know it belonged to you?'

'He's seen it on duty, but that's all. Every nurse wears a watch. He wouldn't have re-membered which nurse wore it, but he knew which wards he had visited,' Petula frowned.

'I should think that anyone who saw this watch would know exactly who wore it. My dear girl, it nearly wore *you*! It's as big as the town hall clock, for heaven's sake!'

He came closer and held the watch within her grasp. Petula took it with relief, but his other hand gripped her wrist.

'Pretty please,' he said. 'It's nice to know that you have fun sometimes. When we were in Tunbridge Wells I got a very different picture. All that Victoriana must be catching and it wouldn't do to be wild on Auntie's territory would it?'

'Please Lou, let me go. You're making a mistake and some day you will know how wrong you are. I don't visit men in their rooms and I am not what Olwen hints about me,' she said firmly.

Lou drew her close and she couldn't escape. When he kissed her tightly compressed lips he found her taut and completely unresponsive. He slackened his grip and looked puzzled. Petula tore away from him and clutched her watch as if it would save her from further insult, but not before she had seen Angus Moray in the doorway with the sheaf of notes he had forgotten to take from the office on his previous visit.

'Don't let me interrupt,' he said coldly and Petula felt as if an icy hand tore at her heart. 'I can see that this ward is far busier than even Sister believes.' He turned away and she ran from the room, pushing past Lou Sheridan and telling him to go away . . . please, go away and leave her in peace.

'Pet?' he called, and his smile died. She was really upset. He started to follow her but decided against it. She wouldn't like Angus seeing her kiss another man. The affair must be hotter than even Olwen Prosser had said.

But now, with Sister Soames and Dr Rosalie Arran on duty, the ward was peaceful and

Petula could concentrate on her work. 'You look a bit pale, too, Nurse,' said Sister.

'I find it difficult to adapt to night duty this time, Sister,' Petula said with truth. Who could sleep during the day when her thoughts were full of the man she loved? A man who would never think of her as anything but a cheap and tawdry piece of colourful rubbish to be thrown out after Christmas. And she hoped that Lou Sheridan would find out how wrong he was about her.

'I've stacked the reports and put the X-rays into this big envelope so they don't slip off the trolley, Sister.'

The older nurse looked at the reports, neatly stacked in a logical sequence, each with the relevant coloured labels and the name, age and address of the patient showing clearly. The red stickers made it clear which of the women were undergoing tests, and Sister nodded approvingly.

'I'll be off now,' said Sister Soames. 'I seem to stay later and later, but it's pleasant to chat and not to rush everything. The women on the balcony are comfortable. I had a chat with all of them earlier. Mrs Bence is a bit too comfortable, I think. Like all those who have little luxury in their lives, she laps up the attention and takes it for granted that she can do as she pleases. She now looks on this ward as a private hotel in which she is a privileged guest, allowed to wander about with a cigarette dangling from her mouth at all hours. The sooner we finish that test, the better it will be for all the ward. She's a menace! I caught her smoking in the general ward and sitting on the end of the bed of a woman who hates the smell of smoke.'

'Not my favourite patient,' said Rosalie Arran.

'It's understandable,' said Sister indulgently. 'At home, she has two huge sons who sit about all day and do nothing but expect to be fed and tolerated until she must be at screaming point. No wonder she has an incipient ulcer.'

'Goodnight, Sister. Are you free to make the round with me, Nurse Howard?' Dr Arran smiled and Petula was forced to admit that she was warm and attractive, with a friendly personality that could have drawn the two girls together easily if they had met under any other circumstances. But she was involved with Angus Moray and was one of his growing collection of women.

I can't become one of a group of camp followers. I refuse to be drawn into a situation that leaves me feeling cheap, thought Petula, but when she watched the gentle profile of the woman doctor, she was puzzled. This was someone with pride and humour and intelligence. There was no trace of sexual self-indulgence in the fine features and soft gaze. Surely there could be no promiscuous relationship between this woman and Dr Moray? But as she pictured him, Petula knew that his influence was such that any woman attracted to him would be as soft as the bubbles floating on a bath of scented water, as sensuous as a massage with aromatic oils—completely in his power if the time was right and the opportunity presented itself.

And last night? She pushed the trolley to the end of the first bed in the ward. Last night he had held her close and his kiss had been more than a light-hearted flirtation. She had known every line of his body and the sudden need he felt for her. If she had clung to him then, he would have won her whole being at whatever time in the future he came to her.

'Mrs Livingstone?' Dr Arran held out her hand for the notes and Petula handed them to her without comment. 'She'll be going home in a day or two,' said the doctor. 'Recovery in a patient after a panic is good for the soul,' said Dr Arran. 'I can't thank Angus enough for making me cope with it. I know how difficult it is to hold back under such conditions, but that man has wonderful control of his feelings.' She spoke softly and with affection, and her tone reminded Petula of the way that Nurse Bolton spoke of the good-looking doctor.

Petula put a hand to her cap. It was pinned too tightly and the pins dragged at the roots of her hair. She removed one clip and it gave her some relief but made the cap feel unsafe. She might end the round with the cap tilted to one side but, with only Dr Arran to see her, she was unlikely to receive any snide remarks. 'Do you need the X-ray viewer, Dr Arran?'

'No, I looked at the X-rays earlier and I know what they say. Dr Moray might want to see them when he comes round later. I know I'm making the round but he wants to check the path reports on the aspirations from yesterday and this morning.'

'He hasn't seen the X-rays?'

'He came to the ward early, before the plates were back from X-ray. He had to take the van for servicing and asked me to cope.' Dr Arran smiled. 'It was his way of leaving me to take charge and to let me know he trusted me.' She walked on to the next bed. 'I know that my decisions are good now and I have a lot more confidence. He's wonderful. Don't you think so?'

'He's a very good doctor,' said Petula.

The first two patients were ready for discharge and their notes showed nothing sinister. 'I've never known so few patients here,' said Rosalie Arran. 'Two went over to surgery today and another three went home. And we aren't admitting until the second week in January, after the next major clinic. Some of the women on the list to come in decided to wait until the children were back at school. So we have empty beds and I can get some study done.'

'The end ward is more crowded than this one,' said Petula.

'I'll take a peep at it,' the doctor said. The ward was so quiet that even a cough sounded loud and when someone sat up to take a drink of orange squash, the sound of fluid pouring into a glass was exaggerated. 'I hate it as quiet as this. I waste a lot of time convincing myself that I'm working,' she smiled.

Nurse Howard knew that the doctor was killing time until her senior registrar might appear. The swing-doors on the outer limits of the ward swished gently and both the girls looked sharply towards the ward entrance, but it was Nurse Bolton, bringing linen from the huge linen baskets left in the corridor by the day staff.

They turned back to the patients and Dr Arran opened the door leading to the balcony ward. The smell of cigarette smoke was far more pronounced than at any time Petula had been in that ward.

Mrs Bence reclined indolently on the spare mattresses which were stacked one on the other by the wall. Petula hid a smile. She looked rather like a Roman senator, with long flowing robes of a nasty shade of mauve, her skimpy fair hair untidy and the smoke from yet another cigarette flowing up between her fingers.

'I think you've smoked enough for one day, Mrs Bence. Sister would like the ward free of smoke for the others to be able to rest.' Dr Arran was pleasant but firm. 'And you don't have to beat the *Guinness Book of Records*, you know. Smoke by all means, but remember that it isn't a good habit and we aren't encouraging you to smoke more, only to show us what effect smoking has on stomach ulcers.'

'I'm nearly out of them until my Herbie brings me some more tomorrow, Doctor. I'll finish this one and get to bed,' the patient said, with an air of doing them a favour.

The others were asleep but, even at rest, Mrs Thomas twitched as if poised for action, the lines on her face much deeper than they should be for a woman of her age.

'The typical gastric type,' whispered Dr Arran as they left the ward. 'If she didn't have something to worry about, she'd invent it, or get upset because she ought to be worrying!'

'I had noticed,' said Petula. 'She checks up on the water-jugs in the ward and we try to tell her that some people are on restricted fluids and aren't allowed an unlimited supply of drinks. Sister said that she could be a menace in the main ward and it's just as well she is restricted to the balcony room.'

They reached the end of the round. Petula wondered why she was on duty. The ward was quiet, the patients were all walking cases who could go to the lavatory alone and needed no bedpans or blanket baths. She had checked water-jugs and tidied tables as they progressed round the beds, and there was no treatment list on the board.

She stifled a yawn. This was terrible! A busy ward was the only antidote to tiredness. The long hours stretched ahead and even with permission to cat-nap in the duty room after midnight, she was unsure if she wanted to do so. Once she had done this and woken shivering and almost disorientated, unable to get warm and with a sick feeling in the pit of her stomach. Was it worth it for an hour of deep sleep?

'Coffee,' said Nurse Bolton firmly. 'We will be asleep on our feet if we don't have strong coffee, every hour, on the hour!' She laughed. 'That will bring them all to the ward, even the surgeons. What it is to have a reputation for hospitality! Have you time to stay, Dr Arran?'

'I'll pop down the corridor to the men and come back in twenty minutes,' said the doctor. 'If Angus comes here first, make him stay. I want a word with him.'

'I'll make a lot of coffee,' said Nurse Bolton. 'You'd better get on with folding linen and checking the list, Nurse Howard.'

'Where do I do that, Nurse?' Petula asked.

'We usually do it in the outside corridor, but I can't have the ward unattended even if there is no really sick patient in there. Take a stretcher trolley from the corridor and use it to put the folded linen in piles, ready for counting. I'll help you to drag in one of the baskets.'

They went outside and managed to bring in one of the heavy baskets, sliding it smoothly over the polished floor. It was peaceful at the balcony end of the main ward and the nurse folding linen could answer bells and keep an eye on all the patients easily. At least it gave Petula something to occupy her hands, even if her mind was in the turmoil that had become its normal state since she had met Dr Angus Moray.

The clean smell of fresh laundry was good after the staleness of the end ward. Even after the windows had been opened, the cigarette smoke persisted and the air fresheners on the window sills had only a partial effect. That woman must smoke like a chimney, thought Petula. She took another pin from her cap to ease the tension on her scalp and when she put it back, the cap still felt unsafe. Damn, I never get it right, she thought. It would have to stay comfortable but unsafe until she went to the duty room again.

The pile of linen mounted and there was a certain satisfaction in doing even this routine work well. The day staff would be pleased to have fresh supplies and none of the chores involved. With the New Year celebrations coming up, everyone wanted as little to do as possible.

It was difficult to think about the Hogmanay dance. It could have been so good. David, her cousin, was coming from Tunbridge Wells with Andy Pershore, the pleasant doctor from the local hospital there, who was to be Petula's partner for the evening. She smiled slightly. If all men could be as uncomplicated as Andy, life would be easy. Andy would never force his attention on a girl—the thought of him kissing her was amusing, to say the least!

The growing feeling between Dulcie and David was the one good thing that had happened during the last week or so, and Petula tried not to think of her own disasters. The dance could have been such fun if Lou Sheridan had stayed as he was at Christmas, instead of talking to Nurse Prosser and believing whatever absurd ideas she told him. Now

he would be very difficult. She shuddered to
visualise Angus Moray's face if Lou was at the
dance, possibly drinking too much and certainly being offensive.

The pile of towels on the trolley seemed
without end as she folded them ready for
packing. Some had been done by the day staff,
but when she looked at the finished product,
Petula discovered that many were folded with
the ends tucked inside, looking very neat but
totally unsuitable for use with sterile forceps.
She re-folded them in the special way that she
had been taught, so that long sterile forceps
could shake out the towel by seizing the two
visible corners and flicking it on to the tray or
trolley in one simple movement, without con-
tamination from fingers or an unsterile object.

Petula tried to concentrate, but one towel
was like another and she was tired. She heard
the sound of the lift when it stopped on the
level of the medical wards and her heart be-
trayed her into knowing that this was what she
both dreaded and yet waited to hear. Her
heart fluttered and all her senses seemed shar-
per. Her hands trembled and one towel fell to
the floor, for she knew that Angus Moray was
expected to come to the ward. The smell of
coffee came as a scented blast from the office
as the door opened and then shut again.

I could go into the balcony ward again, she
thought. But he would go in there and she
wanted to avoid all contact with him. She
wondered where she could be safe from the
probing mockery of the sapphire blue eyes and

the cold smile that told her nothing she wanted to know.

Perhaps the balcony ward *would* be safe—there would be at least one patient awake or drowsing, which would limit what he could say or do to the trivia of normal conversation. Petula folded two more towels, keeping herself to the side of the trolley facing the far office, and poised for flight.

Her senses were certainly honed. She heard each sound from every patient at the far end of the ward and thought she heard the voices from the far office—but that was impossible, unless they were all laughing and talking loudly. A paperback book dropped on the floor and she started as if someone had thrown a brick. She could even hear her own breathing coming in short, painful gasps.

She sniffed. Even her sense of smell was acute. That woman must be smoking again! It was long after lights out and long after Dr Arran had asked her to finish for the day, politely requesting a little consideration for the other people in the ward who didn't smoke.

Nurse Petula Howard moved the trolley further over to the wall to make a wide, free passage to the balcony ward, and decided to stay there until the night round was complete. The door to the office was still shut, indicating that Nurse Bolton was serving coffee to at least one doctor. It would be time for the night superintendent to make her round soon.

Petula slammed a sheet down on to the pile.

That would make three of his women gathered together. Was it possible that they didn't know about the others? Could they really like one another? It was so puzzling. I'm infatuated with the wretched man but I have no intention of being one of his followers, she scolded herself.

She sniffed again. If Mrs Bence was smoking in bed, she must be stopped. Petula pushed the linen basket close to the wall so that it was no hazard to anyone with sheer tights who passed too closely to the rough weave of the sides. She went softly to the door of the balcony room and opened it. The smell of smoke was worse now and the room was full of a hazy greyness. She gasped. The smoke was not coming from one illicit cigarette, but from the side of the ward near the lavatories. The haze deepened and seemed to swell outwards, filling the room. Petula coughed as the acrid stench hit her nostrils, and Mrs Thomas woke up. Remembering her training, Petula instructed her to go and sound the alarm.

With surprising speed, the small woman leaped out of bed and opened the door to the main ward, which Petula had closed after her as she came in.

'Fire, fire!' she shouted as she ran towards the office. And as she ran, leaving the door open, flames erupted in a sheet of intense heat from the two smouldering mattresses that had been propped against the wall.

Mrs Bence lay on her bed, still wearing her dressing-gown over the mauve night-dress.

She was close to the mattresses and her face had an unhealthy colour. She hardly stirred when Petula pulled at her to get her out of bed, and the other two patients now moved as far away from the fire as they could get. Petula glanced at the half-open door and thrust the two women into the main ward. She dragged at Mrs Bence and tried to break her fall as she slipped from the bed. The smoke was getting thicker and Petula looked back towards the fire-escape. There were two options. She could try to drag the woman into the ward and perhaps be overcome by fumes, or she could open the fire-escape door and get her out into the air. Flames licked the wooden table and crept along the skirting-boards. The air from the ward was feeding the fire, and if the flames went past the door, the whole hospital might be in danger. If only there was a fire extinguisher!

Petula fought her way through the smoke to close the ward door. She bolted it so that the only access was through the fire-escape, and ran back to her patient. Sobbing with effort and the growing knowledge that she, too, was becoming affected by the dense smoke, she pulled and pushed the inert form towards the other door.

Dimly she heard the sound of a fire-engine, but it was so faint that she might have imagined it. She pulled again, risking getting closer to the fire, which now sent pools of molten plastic foam from one of the chairs.

Mrs Bence stirred and groaned and, convinced that she was still alive, the nurse was inspired to almost superhuman efforts. The ward door rattled and then footsteps ran away as if someone guessed what she had done. Now they were at the fire-escape door. A wave of nausea and faintness flooded Petula's mind and her hand slipped from the bolt. It would be so easy to rest just for a minute, she thought. It was almost pleasant, this feeling of lassitude that took away the immediacy of the danger . . .

Mrs Bence was heavy and her shoulders lay across the nurse's feet. Try again, and have a rest, Petula mused. She heard voices shouting outside, down below, and thought she saw the flash of a blue light reflected on a distant window. Pretty, she thought. Better than the red flames behind her. She looked up then and, even in her half-consciousness, she felt the heat and knew that she must get out.

She reached for the bolt again and her hand closed over it, pulling it aside. But she had no more strength left. In hospital, everyone wore soft-soled shoes, or they did at the Princess Beatrice Hospital, she thought, shaking her head at the noise that heavy boots were making on the wrought-iron stairs. They'll wake the patients and Night Sister will be cross, she thought . . .

The door was opened with a sudden jerk and hands pulled at the heavy shoulders of the unconscious woman on the floor.

'Take her down,' said a crisp voice. 'No, I can manage the nurse.'

The air was cold after the intense heat of the balcony room and Petula tried to get back into the warm. But the hands that held her seemed made of steel and she fought against the hard chest and the wide shoulder. Dr Angus Moray swore softly and grabbed her, lurching against the solid iron balustrade, and as he turned to carry her down the stairs, her dress caught on the curly Victorian decorations and was ripped, revealing her body, pale and vulnerable.

A sound that was half curse and half moan came to her as the air freshened and she took a deep breath. The arms holding her were safety and warmth and something that she had longed for all her life. She moved closer so that her breasts were crushed against the white coat. A hard button digging into her soft flesh was like a remembered pain that she knew and loved. Her watch was ticking. The big watch that had caused so much trouble was ticking away somewhere near. But it wasn't her watch, it was the urgent beating of a human heart, steady and comforting as the sound of a mother's pulse to a baby.

The shallow steps led to the first landing and Dr Angus Moray stood aside to let the firemen trail the long, snaking coil of hose up to the blazing room. A loud crack told of glass shattering after minutes of intense heat, and Angus ducked, pulling Petula closer against him to protect her from flying fragments and hot ash. A gentle dew of moisture fanned down from the hoses and more glass broke as the cold water came in contact with the heat.

Angus hurried down to the waiting stretchers and Petula felt herself being placed on a clean red blanket. She reached up for the arms that had deserted her and tried to open her eyes. A hand held her wrist and with one eye she saw the wavering lights as a none too gentle finger lifted her eyelid.

'Come on, deep breaths.' The voice was almost harsh in its urgency. She was tired— and what had happened to that wonderful bedside manner that everyone talked about as if it was unique?

'Open your eyes, Petula, open your eyes.' She saw him briefly through narrow slits but the effort was too much. She sighed but the effect was nil. Why didn't they leave her to sleep? 'Rosalie, how is Mrs Bence? Can you leave her and get the oxygen over here?'

'I've sent her up to a side ward for oxygen saturation. I've also written her up for an osmotic diuretic. She's in near coma and I think may have cerebral oedema. Was I right? I thought that it was the quickest way to rid the body of the toxins.'

'Oxygen? Good girl.' A mask was placed over the face of the nurse on the red blanket. Cool air seemed to envelop her as she breathed more and more deeply, suddenly hungry for the air. The mask went away and she opened her eyes to the vivid blue of worried sapphires that slowly warmed in a smile. A leonine head bent to hers and lips that were warm and moulded to her own closed on her mouth in a long kiss. Her eyebrows shot up and she suddenly knew who he was and where they were.

'No,' she said, feebly, but held out her arms to him.

'Yes,' he said, and kissed her again. 'It isn't the one they show in all the good books, Petula, but I like to think it's the kiss of life.'

'There's a bed in the staff ward,' said Dr Arran. 'How is she?'

'Making a remarkably quick recovery. I doubt if she will have complications,' he said, and only Petula saw the devil dancing in the blue eyes.

'I was worried,' said Rosalie Arran. 'I thought I saw you giving mouth to mouth respiration?'

'Just as a precaution,' he said smoothly. 'I'm a great believer in preventive medicine and it did stimulate her after a burst of oxygen.' He stood away from the trolley. 'She can go up to the ward now, until we check that everything is in place.'

Petula put a hand to cover her breasts, inadequately held by the bra of coffee-coloured silk and lace that was part of a set of good lingerie given to her at Christmas. She pulled at the blanket to cover her and stared at him. If he didn't know that everything was 'in place', as he so kindly said, then no one did!

The trolley rumbled over the rough grass and the texture of the blanket tickled her bare flesh. She was still vaguely light-headed and wanted to laugh and cry by turns. Angus

Moray admitted that he had stimulated her to make her come back to consciousness. He had done what any man would do to shock her into being. She licked her dry lips as if to taste his kiss. Even those kisses were made to shock, to force her to look at him and to come back to normal.

She took more deep breaths, knowing now that this was essential to her progress, and by the time the lift stopped by the side ward of the female surgical block she had a blinding headache, but was no longer in need of any help, or kisses . . .

The night superintendent hovered by the bed while Petula drank a pint of orange squash. She smiled. 'That's good. You look better each time I come to look at you.' She lifted up the empty jug. 'I'll get some more, unless you'd rather have another colour? The flavour of the orange squash is the same as the grapefruit and the lemon, in my opinion. They add a little more citric acid to the others, that's all.'

'I don't mind what it is. I know I have to drink plenty and I'm thirsty enough to do as I'm told, Sister.' Petula sat up in bed and smiled. To get to know Beatties from the other side of the blanket, so to speak, was a revelation.

Swept along on a tide of comfort and efficiency, she now knew how a patient felt on admission, especially if she was tired and feeling depressed. The machinery of help and healing went into action and a strange sensation of well-being and perfect trust took the place of anxiety and perhaps even hopelessness. To be a part of that help would mean even more now that she understood it fully. She poured another drink as soon as the fresh jug appeared.

'How is Mrs Bence?' she said, half dreading the reply. 'I tried to get her out, Sister, but she was so heavy.'

'You did all the right things, Nurse Howard. Even the firemen found that she was quite a handful to get down to the ambulance.' Sister Tyler smiled. 'It sounds odd, doesn't it, to have ambulances waiting to rescue people from a hospital?'

'I was so afraid that the fire would spread. I didn't know what to do at first, until I saw that the flames were going towards the main ward,' Petula confided.

'Mrs Thomas gave the alarm. Nurse Bolton thought she had flipped when she ran into the office screaming! But it gave us time to ring the brigade and to alert other wards. The few patients in the main ward have gone to the old isolation block until tomorrow. Then they're going to that rather nice ward next to Childrens' that we were keeping for observation. But positively no smoking there!'

'I should have found it earlier, Sister. I could smell the cigarette smoke and thought it was just the smell that we had noticed before they all went to bed,' Petula said.

'Mrs Bence didn't go to bed until she had finished reading a magazine, according to Mrs

Thomas. She was smoking while she sat on the mattresses and then went to lie on her bed, leaving the cigarette-end on the side of the mattress, resting on the ashtray. As it burned down, it fell on to the mattress and smouldered. By the time you came to the rescue Mrs Bence had inhaled a lot of carbon monoxide.' Sister Tyley smiled. 'Thanks to the prompt action of everyone, including you and Dr Arran, she is very much better.'

'Is she unconscious?' Petula asked with interest.

'No, she was only on the brink when we found her and should make a full recovery. It will be a sobering lesson to everyone. She will never leave a lighted cigarette again and it might even help her to give up the habit for good. The hospital authorities who have wavered a little about making firm rules about smoking here will step up their precautions, and places like the balcony wards will have better fire-fighting appliances as permanent items on the inventory.' Petula thought that Sister Tyley looked rather pleased about that.

'I suppose I should have run back to the main ward for a fire-extinguisher.' She put down her glass and looked guilty. 'But it never entered my head. I was far too busy trying to move Mrs Bence.'

'The smoke wouldn't let you think clearly, even if you had time to use the extinguisher. No, the only way to deal with a sudden out-break like that is to have efficient sprinklers in the ceiling. Difficult with a glass roof like the balcony, but they'll have to think of something.' Sister Tyley took the rather limp hand on the bed and felt for the pulse. 'A lot better. Drink up and you should be quite well in a day or so,' she smiled comfortingly.

'I'm fine now, Sister. I could go back on duty.'

'After all that fluid, you will be trotting off to the loo quite often.' Sister laughed. 'Try your legs—I think you'll find that drinking and making that short walk is about your limit for a while!' She looked at her watch. 'I ought to check a few patients, but I'll come and see you before I go off duty again.'

'Is Dr Arran off duty now? She ought to get some sleep,' said Petula, but what she really wanted to know was if Dr Angus Moray was awake and likely to come to see her.

'I packed her off to bed and told Dr Moray to go, too.' Sister glanced at the cylinder of oxygen by the bed. 'Ring if you have the slightest cause to worry, won't you? I don't think that you will need that, but we don't want to have to administer artificial respiration in any form, do we?' Her pretty mouth turned up at the corners in what could be described as a roguish smile, and she left the girl in bed staring after her and blushing.

Dr Moray had told her that he had kissed her! He must have done so, unless Dr Arran had mentioned it. It was just too puzzling. If the women in his life could laugh when the man they loved kissed another woman as she lay nearly naked and helpless, they must be slightly odd.

Petula tried to stand and had to clutch at the bed to save herself from falling. She tried to walk and found that a chair pushed in front of her was the best form of propulsion. She giggled slightly, recalling an aunt who complained that one glass of sherry was fine, two was lovely, but three went straight to her knees. I'm drunk on smoke and orange squash, she thought and when she came back from the toilet she was weak and glad to slip into bed. One more glass of liquid and a rest and I'll be fighting fit, she thought, but there was no rush, was there?

Mornings in surgical wards start early, as Petula soon discovered. She woke with a start, thinking that it was still the middle of the night, but aware of the muted bustle in the ward next door. She drank some more squash, although her thirst was not as great as it had been before she fell asleep. She moved her legs and arms and found them stronger.

She sighed. All this drinking made her trot, as Sister had hinted. She swung her legs over the edge of the bed and stood, cautiously holding on to the bed-table. Her legs felt better but still wobbly. At least I should be able to get there and back without a chair. I'm a bit young for a Zimmer frame, she thought, and her pride made her try to walk without aid.

She clutched her dressing-gown round her firmly, blessing the fact that someone had fetched her own things from her room and she was not wearing hospital clothes. Thank you, Aunt Sophie, she thought, as she belted the soft silk kimono, with the trailing embroidery of mimosa on the dull green back, over the matching night-dress. They'd been gifts from her most imaginative and generous aunt, who she saw only rarely but who never failed to give her something breathtaking.

Petula brushed her hair from her eyes and started for the door. It was a long way without a chair to rest against. She made the outward trip safely and stayed to regain her breath and poise before going back.

All right, she told herself, crossly. So you made a mistake and you were too pigheaded to know your own limitations. The ward was busy as the staff prepared three patients for morning surgery and the rest of the night staff were feverishly making beds. There was a bell push in the loo, but Petula couldn't bring a nurse away just to help her back to bed. It was unfair to be a bother to an already overworked ward.

She straightened her shoulders and began to walk. First, she could get to the window sill outside the lavatory block and then make a move towards the door to her room. Once inside, she could clutch the chair she had abandoned as she left the room. From there it was easy.

The window sill offered little support. It was too high to sit on and too narrow to lean on with any safety—and the kimono was slippery. Petula paused and breathed deeply, remembering that this was one of her exercises.

That was the answer. She felt much better. The door was shut, although she had left it half-open. A passing nurse, thinking she didn't want to be disturbed, must have shut it carefully as she passed. Petula opened it and pushed the door wide. The chair had gone and her bed was tidy. The chair now sat neatly aligned to the wall where it belonged.

'Damn efficient nurses,' she said.

The floor looked slippery and the bed a long way off. She took more deep breaths and then wondered if she was over-breathing! Her heart was pumping hard and her knees wouldn't carry her. She heard a step behind her and half turned, which was a mistake, for she lost her balance.

'What the hell do you think you are doing? Get into bed at once!' Dr Angus Moray lifted her from the ungainly heap she made on the floor. A glimmer of humour lit the stern eyes and turned into a reluctant twinkle. 'Do I have to spend my life scooping you off the floor?' he said. He lifted her with almost insulting ease, as if she was a feather of no particular importance, and placed her on the top of the bedclothes.

'I was managing very well until you startled me,' Petula said, with great dignity.

'Pity. I was all set to give you the kiss of life again,' he murmured. She saw that his eyes were tired and a pulse beat deeply in his temple. That pulse-beat had comforted her as he brought her to safety. She blushed.

'You don't recall much of last night, do

you?' He seemed cautious, as if he hoped that she had forgotten.

'It's all a bit hazy,' she lied.

'But I have to find out what you remember.'

Was he mocking her, or was he now the doctor? He turned away to the tray she hadn't noticed. 'I have to test your reflexes,' he said.

'I'm all right.' She sat up and tried to untuck the efficiently folded bedclothes so that she could slip under the covers—but as she was lying on top of them, it was impossible.

'I must,' he said in a tone that would take no refusal. He bared her feet and ran a wooden probe along the soles of each one, making her toes curl with more than the usual response. He raised his eyebrows.

'Brisk,' he said. He pushed up the silky night-dress above her knees and selected a small patella hammer from the items on the tray. His hand under her knee, making it flex slightly, made her want to shake—but she bit her lip and controlled herself.

'Too tense,' he said, and smiled. 'Relax, I'm unlikely to hurt you.' He struck the knee briefly and her reaction was good.

'Now the other.' He slid his hand under the other knee and it lingered after the test was over. Petula was intensely aware of soft silk and the pressure of the man's hand on her leg, and his nearness. She took a long, shuddering breath.

'Nothing wrong with your breathing now,' he said. He looked down at the soft curves under the clinging silk and put the stethoscope he was holding back in his pocket. His voice was rough with an emotion that could have been anger or desire.

'Tell Rosalie that I did most of the tests but left her to go over the rest,' he muttered.

At the door he bumped into Dr Arran, murmured something and hurried away. The doctor raised her eyebrows.

'What gives with Angus? He said I was to go over your chest as he was in a hurry. He seemed a bit *distrait*.'

She took Petula's tense hand from the bed and felt for the pulse. 'Feeling all right? Pulse is a bit up, but good and strong. She slipped the stethoscope wings into her ears and motioned to Petula to undo her nightdress. She smiled as she completed the examination.

'Not a thing wrong that a day in bed won't cure.' She made a note on the chart and looked at her patient keenly. 'Angus is a stickler for protocol. Just as well, as it's so easy for a man to indulge in unethical behaviour—not that he has ever been guilty of that, but that night-dress *is* rather fetching.' She waved from the door, as if she had not noticed the hot blush that suffused the face of the girl on the bed.

CHAPTER SIX

'I FELT an absolute fraud the day after it happened,' said Petula. 'At first, my legs seemed made of spaghetti, but that soon went and I was left with a headache and a slight feeling of depression.'

'Is depression a feature of carbon monoxide poisoning?' asked Juno.

'It was with me,' said Petula with feeling. But how much was due to the accident and how much to the fact that she had seen nothing of Angus Moray since the early morning, when he had tested her reflexes and then left her abruptly to the care of his house physician, she wouldn't admit. 'Anyway, I'm over it now and feel as if I'm not entitled to the extra day off that they seem to think I should take.'

'Make the most of it. You've had a glimpse of Surgical and you will need all your strength when you go there on day duty,' Juno laughed.

Olwen Prosser sat in the cane chair by the window and put her feet on the table, making the chair creak and groan in an irritating way. The sitting-room in the nurses' home was sunlit and warm, although outside a cold wind flurried the dead leaves and threatened snow. The girls, in their thin cotton uniforms, watched the sun on the window and thought of

129

spring, but there was a lot a winter waiting to be experienced before the air outside would be warm enough for them to go out without the thick, scarlet-lined blue cloaks that made winter bearable.

'It's lucky for some,' Olwen said. 'Everyone making a fuss about you, when all you did was pass out.'

'She tried to save her patients and she might even have saved a lot of the hospital from going up in flames,' said Juno reproachfully. 'I talked with the doctor and she said that even the firemen were impressed by Petula's quick thinking.'

'And did a handsome fireman put you over his shoulder to bring you to safety?' said Olwen.

'She wouldn't know who brought her down,' said Dulcie quickly.' I doubt if Pet remembers anything of importance.'

'Dr Sheridan couldn't tell me anything,' Olwen admitted with obvious dissatisfaction. 'He said he was out of the hospital and didn't see the fire, so how could he be expected to know what happened.' She frowned. 'He hasn't been as friendly as he was before he went on holiday with you, Pet.'

'Correction. He went to see his friend at the hospital in Tunbridge Wells and we happened to have mutual acquaintances there,' said Dulcie. Her eyes were over-bright, as if she was really annoyed, and Petula thought she knew the cause. It would be very embarrassing for Dulcie if Olwen put two and two together and made a hundred when David came to the dance.

'By the way,' said Petula. 'I hope you don't mind, Dulcie, but when my cousin rang up about the dance, I had to say that you would be partnering him and not me. It wouldn't be fair to bring him all this way to London just to have a feeble woman unable to help him enjoy the evening.' She smiled. 'So, do me a favour and take him off my hands. I think his friend is coming just for the social aspect of the evening.' It wasn't strictly true, but it was good enough for the twitching ears of Olwen.

'Is Dr Sheridan going?' she asked.

'Yes, Olwen, he'll be there playing the bagpipes,' said Dulcie.

'You have to be joking!' said Olwen crossly, and went away full of offended dignity.

'She doesn't believe the truth but she believes every rumour in the hospital,' Dulcie laughed.

'Does he really play the bagpipes?' Juno was wide-eyed and laughing. 'That I *would* like to hear. That man has so many hidden talents!'

'If he plays as badly as he did in Tunbridge, all the hospital will hear him,' said Dulcie with feeling. 'But it gives him a lot of pleasure to write about it to his folks in Canada.'

'I hope I don't spoil the fun,' said Petula. 'I don't think I shall be able to dance every dance, but I'll try. I brought all my stuff back with me and there is enough spare for you to borrow, Dulcie.'

Dulcie blushed. 'I bought a kilt,' she said.

'You never know, I might like Scottish dancing so much that I shall want to join a club.'

'I know a club wanting fresh talent,' said Petula. 'I'll mention it to David.'

'He already knows,' said Dulcie. 'He said he'd arrange it.'

So life was taking a tender curve towards love for Dulcie! Petula was delighted, but her pleasure in the happiness of two nice people was overshadowed by a veil of regret. Why couldn't life be less complicated for her? Why must I fall for the one man who could never make any woman happy for a lifetime? she sighed.

She busied herself with her handbag, which had a loose clasp, and tried to hide her trembling lips. The memory of Angus Moray's lips, warm and firm on her own mouth, was still vivid and painful. The recognition of his masculinity and the sensual touch of his fingers on her body were unforgettable. She dreaded being with him again and knew that if he touched her the flame would burn clear and bright in her heart and her love would show in her eyes. And yet she must steel her heart against his machismo, his terrifying sexuality.

He was going away soon for a break, and she had not seen him since . . . that time. Perhaps he was already away with his woman, making love and forgetting that he had kissed a junior nurse.

But please, don't laugh at the memory, don't boast of the time when you gave kisses to revive a fainting girl, she pleaded silently. She blushed, imagining him talking to other men, mentioning it as a victory, one of the perks of an intimate job . . .

'No!' she said. Dulcie looked at her with some anxiety. 'Oh, don't take any notice of me,' said Petula, shakily. 'I'm still a bit vague and talk to myself.' She picked up her coat. 'I'm going to have a long, deep bath and get changed. David will be here soon and we ought to be ready.'

She went to her room listlessly, wishing that she had not arranged to go to the dance. What had she to celebrate as the new year took over from the old? But she regretted her thoughts about Angus Moray. It was unjust to think of him talking about her in that way. Everyone knew that he was perfectly correct in his professional manner and would never risk his reputation by indulging in unethical behaviour. She looked with blank eyes at the towel on the hook and washed her face for the second time. So if he was being professional, that kiss had been just shock treatment, a prescription as cold and calculated as if he was writing her up for a simple cough remedy.

The soft woollen kilt fell in well-cut folds over her slim hips and the silky blouse sent a cascade of frills over her gently swelling bosom. She was pale, but that could be explained by the ordeal that she had endured and no one would expect her to look one hundred per cent fit. She took her hospital cape as the most practical covering for the clothes and went to find Dulcie.

Juno was watching Dulcie add the final touches to her perfect make-up. Petula almost wished that she had taken more trouble to cover her pallor, but Duclie had an inner bloom that would have been enough to give her a glow impossible to achieve with cosmetics.

'Shall we go? I believe we are to wait in the hall of the medical school and they'll pick us up there.'

'Did David call?' asked Petula.

'Yes, he said he'd be here at eight.' Dulcie smiled. 'He did ask for you, but I happened to be by the phone.'

'Fine,' said Petula and felt even more excluded from the warmth, as if someone had taken her favourite seat by the fire. It would be easy to cry. She gave a wry smile as they walked to their rendezvous.

David was there, smiling. Dulcie looked disappointed.

'He's a coward,' said Petula. 'He hates wearing the kilt, but he compromises by buying well-cut trews.'

'I couldn't outshine Andy,' said David. 'And you haven't had the traumatic experience of viewing my knees. Not a pretty sight,' he added.

'So all the men will be in trews? How dull,' said Dulcie.

'Not all. Get a load of that,' said David.

Lou Sheridan came towards them, almost hidden under a mass of lace and velvet and bright tartan. He carried his bagpipes under one arm and looked about him with glowing pride. Behind him, as if she was slightly over-awed by the bright spectacle, came Delia Tyley in a simple kilt and plain white shirt and a band of tartan across one shoulder. She looked very beautiful and Petula knew that many men must be attracted to her.

Sister Tyley smiled at the young nurse who had only just been allowed to join in the social life of the hospital after the fire, and Petula smiled back, noticing that, far from being overawed, the night superintendent was amused and somewhat embarrassed by the doctor in tartan. It was a Scottish celebration, but he stood out like a man wearing a ten-gallon hat to church.

'Lou has done his nut!' she whispered. 'I hope that he doesn't try to play that thing.'

'There's a group and a piano and violin for the more formal Scottish dancing,' said Dulcie. 'Maybe we could sabotage it!'

'Where's Angus?' asked Delia. 'He said he'd be here at eight and I know that his wards are slack and covered by a stand-in for the night.'

Petula tugged at her belt and wondered if she could plead tiredness so early in the evening. She felt her resolve ebbing. She couldn't face him now. But as she turned, she saw him standing at one side of the door, watching the rest of the group assemble. He was serious, and the deep blue eyes gave away no feeling. His hair gleamed with brushing and good health, but the recalcitrant lock that always threatened to fall over his brow, did so in spite of discipline.

His shirt was plain and white with a small ruffle, and the Murray tartan of his kilt was subdued and elegant. In his sock the skean-dhu looked at home, not the fancy dress addition worn by Lou Sheridan.

Petula stared, and he saw how pale she was above the diagonal fall of the scarlet and black Innes tartan. He came towards her slowly. 'Are you fit to be here?' he asked.

'Of course. I shall be on duty in two days' time.'

He frowned. She had sounded off-hand and defensive. 'Are you entitled to wear that?'

'What do you mean?' she replied.

He glanced at Lou with a mixture of irritation and amusement. 'Some people just pick a tartan because it matches the decor.' He looked down at her, touching the plaid on her shoulder briefly. 'Innes? For a Howard?'

'David did the research and I take his word that we are entitled to wear it,' she said shortly. 'And Dulcie bought it because she likes something subdued.'

'Welcome to the clans,' he said and leaned forward to kiss her cheek. She drew back as if he had scalded her.

'I think that Sister Tyley is asking for you,' she said. Dr Moray regarded her coldly, inclined his head as if taking his leave, and left her without another glance. She watched him go, loving every movement of his taut body and his air of confident superiority, wearing the kilt as if born to it.

If only he was not a man who took women and then discarded them when he had taken what he wanted. If only she was the kind of girl who welcomed such advances and could love a little, take passion when it offered and have no regrets when the heat of desire faded and left nothing except the need to go on to more conquests and fresh kicks . . .

'They want to get started,' said Andy, David's friend, coming to her with a smile. 'Feeling strong enough to partner me, Pet?'

'If you promise to scoop me up if I fall by the wayside,' she said. He was friendly and comforting, with none of the threat or promise of a grand passion. I ought to marry a man like him, she thought, feeling easy in his company and knowing that he would never expect miracles from anyone.

He stood in place, listening for the opening bars of a schottische, a slow polka that would get everyone loosened up for the more energetic dances. On the other side of the room, Angus Moray was dancing with Delia Tyley. Many of the dances and the groups who had come to join in the ordinary dance programme watched them, too, seeing a perfect match of co-ordinated dancing and good looks.

Petula concentrated on her own steps and began to enjoy herself more than she thought possible. Andy was fun, the atmosphere was festive and even Lou Sheridan seemed less brash now that other tartans abounded among the dancers. Dulcie was radiant and the bond between her and David showed.

The music stopped and they made for the bar. Andy insisted on fetching some of the delicious punch that was the contribution of the wife of one of the surgeons, and several of the couples gravitated towards each other.

'How is it?' said Delia, smiling. 'Just the thing to aerate the lungs!'

'Quite a gentle start,' said Petula. 'I was surprised how much I remembered.' She looked up and into the blue eyes that threatened to break her heart. Dr Angus Moray sipped red wine cup and didn't smile.

'Do you often dance like this?' said Petula, to break the silence.

'Not very often,' said Delia. 'So little time for everything, and although I love dancing, I have limited opportunity.' She smiled. 'Angus is very good. I shall have to opt out when they announce the sword dance. In fact, I shall dance only the simple ones.'

'We ought to swop partners, Delia.' Andy thrust a full glass of punch into Petula's hands. 'I have a sneaking suspicion that my partner is far too good for me and I know I wouldn't dare dance with sharp blades lying around on the floor ready to amputate my feet!'

They all laughed and even Angus smiled and relaxed. 'Even you couldn't be that clumsy,' said David. Lou joined them, drink in hand. 'I wonder what you want now? The band has already tactfully refused your services and we have a real player coming to pipe in the New Year,' he teased.

'I want a partner for the next dance.' Lou was glassy-eyed and the tumbler he held was half full of what looked like neat whisky. He looked at Petula and smiled fatuously. 'You promised me a dance, Petula, and I claim it now.'

'Sorry,' said a smooth but firm voice. 'She's booked for the next few dances. Why not wait for the Gay Gordons and ask one of the pretty nurses over there to dance with you?' Under the even tones was a solid resolve and Lou couldn't argue.

'Maybe I'll do just that.' He walked away to the bar and Angus smiled politely.

'I hope you weren't dying to dance with him? I felt that you were in no fit state to cope with Lou after he's been at the malt.' He listened to the music starting again. 'Can you do this?' Petula nodded, and in a dream followed him to the middle of the floor where four couples were ready in two groups.

'Come on, I did teach you how it went,' said David, and dragged an apprehensive Dulcie to join Angus and his nervous partner. Petula looked at him gratefully. The fact that Dulcie was an amateur would help her to relax, as they all tried to finish the dance successfully.

Two swords were crossed on the floor and the dancing began. Petula held her back straight and her hands high in a graceful curve as she stepped daintily and precisely between the gleaming blades. The line of her hips was gentle and the kilt flowed smoothly over her slim legs. She watched the man who partnered her and their glances locked as they went through the intricacies of the dance. A ribbon of consciousness formed and glowed between them, sweet as desire and as delicate as a cobweb. The others stood back to watch and Dulcie held the hand of the man she loved, knowing that something important was forming between the expert dancers.

'That was superb,' said Angus. He took Petula's hand and raised it to his lips in a gesture that would have been impossible if he was dressed in anything but the graceful but very masculine garments he wore. The froth of fine lace at his wrist brushed her hand in a secondary kiss and she trembled with awareness and tried to hide it in breathlessness.

'You dance very well,' she said.

'I had no idea that we had such talent between us.'

'We ought to give exhibitions,' she said and laughed. 'But I'm very glad that I didn't have Lou as a partner.'

'He would never do as your partner,' Angus said, and his lips twitched although he sounded serious. Petula longed for him to bend and kiss her mouth. The agony of being with him was growing. I don't care if he is as I think, I want him more than I've wanted anyone in my life, she told herself. The tension grew.

'They are playing something more generally known,' he said, quietly.

'So you should dance with Sister Tyley,' she said.

'No, she seems happy enough without me.' He took her hand but she drew away slightly. 'It's either me or Lou,' he whispered, and Petula followed him to the dance floor. Glancing back, there was no sign of Lou. Angus laughed and drew her close, to the beat of an old-fashioned waltz. Colours flashed by as they whirled to the music and her head went back, the bright hair fanning out as her ribbon came adrift. 'That reminds me. I have one of your caps.' Angus looked down into her face. 'You lost it the night of the fire. Do you want it back?'

'Yes, of course I do. I have to account for all my uniform,' she said. 'Thank you for keeping it safe.'

'It was my pleasure.'

'And thank you . . . I haven't thanked you for saving me. At least, I don't think I have.' She was confused under the intense gaze, gabbling like an idiot because she had to say something, anything, to make him look away and not to generate this sensation of falling, losing herself in a deep pool of surrender. His hands on her waist sent exquisite shudders of ecstasy up her spine and her lips parted softly as if in anticipation of his kiss.

'It was an experience I wouldn't have missed or given to any other man,' he said, and she was mentally naked under his gaze. Under the thin shirt she wore the same brief underwear that had survived the fire and she had the ridiculous notion that he could see through her clothes.

The music stopped but enthusiastic clapping made the band leader shrug and raise his baton once more. Gently, the strains of an old tune began. The lights dimmed and the pace was sedate and sensual as only the close dancing of the slow foxtrot can be.

'This is pretty old stuff,' said Petula in an effort to deride the dance.

'They had a very good thing going when they had formal ballroom dancing,' he said. His body was close to hers, his hands at her back, bringing her closer, ever closer.

'The modern dances may be almost tribal and erotic in their way, but this is better.'

Petula gasped, feeling his hands slip over her waist, one to her shoulders and one to her gently undulating hips. She was breathless, with every fibre of her body alerted to his touch, to his nearness and the tight muscles under the kilt. His breath on her hair was a butterfly, his lips on her cheek a dream. She danced as if no floor existed, floating on his direction, a part of his being, her body almost fused with his.

Was it years later that the music stopped, or only a minute? The lights went up and the dancers groaned their displeasure, but as if the band felt puritanical and guilty at making such a romantic atmosphere, they changed direction and speed to the Gay Gordons—and moments later the floor was full of laughing, wildly gyrating bodies, twirling and dipping and having fun. It was a blessed release and Petula laughed with the rest, wondering what she might have said or done if she had been lost in her dream for much longer.

The evening was an obvious success. The mixture of dancing suited most couples and the fact that this was New Year's Eve lent an added excitement. 'What have you decided will be your New Year resolutions?' Angus was by her side again as soon as the buffet supper was over.

'Should I make any?' She smiled rather sadly. How can I tell you what I feel? How can I tell you that I am not the girl I was two months ago, and that I no longer care what comes in the future? Without you, I have no plans but my work, and that has lost its place in my ambitions, she thought.

'Everyone can improve a corner of his life,' he said. 'We all do and say things that we would rather not have done. And I know that I have to do many things that I have not had the courage to do in the old year.'

She glanced up, expecting him to be laughing. But his blue eyes were intensely serious and she drew in her breath sharply, wondering at what she saw there, not daring to accept the promise that lay behind the words.

'I know. I have been stupid so many times,' she whispered. It was easy to forget her doubts about this man and to think that he was incapable of everything she had known to be true. These steadfast blue eyes could never deceive a woman, could they? A roll of drums followed by a showy exhibition on all the tympani drew a laugh and the full attention of the crowd, and the words that hovered were left unsaid, but quivered in the air like a precious gift. They were delayed, but surely they would be given, with joy, later?

'Ladies and gentlemen, we are approaching the witching hour, the hour when we leave the old and embrace the new. Charge your glasses. Gather round to toast the New Year.'

Petula took the offered glass and looked up through protecting eyelashes. Would he give up the old loves for her? Was the tender promise of those eyes for real? The chimes from the church clock down the road came clearly through the open window that had been flung wide as the midnight hour drew near. As they sounded, car horns hooted and in the medical school couples kissed, turned to other partners and kissed again, and to others once more, laughing and drinking, wishing joy and prosperity and success to everyone in a sudden upsurge of communal affection.

Someone shut the window again and the room was cosy once more as arms were linked, the music played and voices took up the theme of *Auld Lang Syne*.

Petula had been kissed by at least six men, including Lou Sheridan, who was now rosily unaware of any dancing ambitions and any thoughts of piping in the New Year. Angus was torn away by giggling females and managed only an apologetic and agonised glance towards the small girl with the pale face and haunted expression before regaining his poise and doing his Scottish duty, kissing every woman in reach and drinking the dram handed to him.

As the old year was driven out, Petula tried to clutch at its ragged coat-tails and to retain a little of the comfort and familiarity it had given her. Before her stretched an unknown era, filled with glittering possibilities that might never be fulfilled. She saw Angus kissing Sister Tyley, his expression tender and easy as if they knew each other very well indeed, and the doubts of the old year threatened to push past the gate into the new, clean, untried year ahead.

Dulcie and David came to her with the news of their engagement, which she had expected and welcomed, and as they kissed her, she had tears in her eyes. She looked up, but Angus was gone. Among all the women in the room, surely she alone had not received a kiss from the man she loved. Lou came to her shamefaced.

'Angus said sorry.'

'Sorry for what? For walking off with my watch?' Her tone was chilly. Lou was flushed and unsteady on his feet and the false glow that had surrounded him all the evening when he was drinking and flirting with whoever would dance with him was ebbing fast.

'Don't be like that, Pet,' he said uneasily. 'I'm sorry.'

'That makes two of you saying you are sorry, but neither of you tells me why you need to be,' she snapped.

'I know now that it was a mistake. Angus

took your watch by mistake—how was I to know?' He looked belligerent. 'Nurse Prosser seemed so sure.'

'And you believed her.' Petula turned away. Angus was gone without even a goodbye and she had been kissed by all the men around her but not by him.

'Petula, listen to me.' Lou frowned as if his mind wasn't all that clear. 'He told me to tell you that he had a case to see. It was really a message for me about a guy with mixed symptoms. Might be medical and might be surgical. Vague pains and high temp and odd symptoms.' Lou shook his head to rid his thought processes from the excess of spirits. He loosened the expensive cravat. 'They said they'd send him to surgical and would I examine, but Angus heard and said he'd take it.'

'He's a physician, not a surgeon. Haven't you got your lines crossed, Lou?'

'No, Angus said I was pissed and couldn't make any worthwhile decision. He was very rude. When he went, he said to tell you. I'm sorry he had to leave the party, Pet. Sorry if I broke it up.'

'There was nothing personal to break up,' she said. She recalled that Sister Tyley had gone, too. She was off duty but she had left at the same time as the medical registrar. Was it just coincidence or couldn't she bear to let him go after being kissed so tenderly?

Petula frowned. Sisters had certain advantages. Delia Tyley could wander about the hospital in her off duty clothes and there would be no comment. No one would question her right to go into the ward with Dr Moray. Rank mattered even in affairs of the heart, it seemed.

'He did say he'd see you soon,' said Lou, brightening. 'He was quite sure about that. He has to be away for a while, starting tomorrow. He's got it all ready, you see,' he said as if she needed placating. 'Nice trip to see his birds. Got the old waggon all set and good luck to him.' Lou stood up shakily. 'I think I ate something bad,' he said and walked unevenly to the door.

Petula fetched her cloak and glanced back at the nearly empty room. It had all been said, the good luck wishes and the hopes for the future. The band had packed up and the dais was littered with beer cans and paper plates, reminding her of the debris of the Christmas decorations.

Andy hovered near, sensing that something had gone wrong, but he only smiled and offered to walk her home. Dulcie and David had vanished and, in any case, Petula didn't wish to intrude on the limited time they had left during this visit. She stepped out into the darkness and heard stifled giggles in the shadows where two couples were closely entwined, and she tried to ignore their laughter.

Angus Moray hadn't changed. In spite of his sudden anxiety and his sexual need of her, he was still the same. Sister Tyley would be with him now while he examined his patient, and then what? He was all set to take her away for a break.

Petula looked across to the car park as they came to the nurses' home. A large dark shadow against the walls showed the camper-van, all ready to leave in the morning, to go who knew where?

She tried to smile and to talk about the dancing and about Dulcie and David, and she knew that Andy thought that he bored her. She couldn't tell him that she thought he was one of the nicest men she'd met, but that the man she loved was going away with a woman and her heart was breaking.

'Goodnight, Pet,' he said. Impulsively, she kissed his cheek and smiled.

'I feel so tired, Andy. I'm not as fully re-covered as I believed. I'm sorry not to be more fun, but I'm dead on my feet.'

'I understand,' he said. 'Goodbye, Petula. It was nice meeting you.' Her heart was heavy as she went into her room. Nice men like Andy got few of the breaks in this life, while men like Angus Moray lifted an imperious little finger and had women falling over each other to be with him.

CHAPTER SEVEN

'THEY SOON got the rubble cleared,' said Juno. 'But I suppose it's a priority as the ambulances come through this way.'

Petula looked up at the huge sheets of plastic which protected the end of the ward where once the Victorian balcony had hung with its thick glass walls and ornate wrought-iron stairs. Tiny sparkles of broken glass still showed where the bulk of the blazing area had collapsed and the lavatory block was exposed, poised against the remaining wall, the pipes hanging in a grotesque mass over the strangely untouched lavatory pedestal. It reminded Petula of photographs of bomb-damaged London during the war, when whole rooms were open to the sky, showing pathetic remnants of furniture, beds balanced on girders and wallpaper that was never meant for outdoor viewing.

Petula drew her thick cloak about her and shivered. It was bitterly cold. A glance at the car park showed that the camper-van was still away after three days. Life went on in the hospital and the Princess Beatrice seemed unmoved by the near tragedy that had threatened her. Already, the medical ward was in operation in another block and the old ward would be redecorated, improved and re-equipped to the advantage of staff and patients. They went back into the building.

'It seems odd to be working during the day,' said Petula.

'But better, would you say?'

'Yes.'

'You don't sound very certain.' Juno looked worried. 'Are you sure that you are fit for duty? You look very pale and I think that you hear about half of what I say.'

'I'm fine, really I am.' Petula took a deep breath. 'See, I can fill my lungs without coughing, I can run and I'm eating everything I see!' Juno hurried after her, puffing as she tried to catch up.

'You don't have to prove it. I believe you,' she said, taking off her cloak as soon as the warmth of the main hospital hit them.

Petula waved goodbye and walked slowly to the stairs. Men in a surgical ward were quite a different experience. The ward was very busy now, full of fresh admissions after the holiday period, but it couldn't only be the change from nursing women to nursing men and the change from night to day shifts that made her feel so detached from everything.

She put a hand up to her cap. It was becoming a habit and she was almost surprised to find it securely in place. Dr Angus Moray had taken her cap from the muddy steps when she lost it the night of the fire, and she must get it back or have to account for it to the admin people.

He could have left it in her letter space in the

nurses' home. He often passed by and even came in to visit doctors who were living there in the staff flatlets.

But she had not had a sight of him. If he was away, it was obvious that he couldn't bother with one soiled cap. But there had been time before he left to . . . to what? To ring her up and tell her he loved her? Petula hurried along the corridor. To leave the cap with a friendly message that he had enjoyed dancing with her?

'Hey, don't you say hello to old friends?' She turned to see Lou Sheridan grinning at her. 'I hear that you are with us now. About time we stole a few pretty women from Angus!' He matched his step to hers. 'He's a genius with the girls. As soon as he gets an intelligent girl either in his firm or on the ward, he makes damn sure she has at least one weekend free to give exclusively to him.' He sighed. 'Wish I had his luck, charm, or whatever convinces them that a weekend out there is a glorious experience.'

'And has he taken someone this weekend?'

'Delia has gone this time and I think that Ros is manning the guns in a week or so. I tried to muscle in for a spell but we didn't get on very well. The girls said I was too rough and made a lot of noise.'

He lifted a hand in salute and disappeared into the side ward and Petula went to report to Sister. To her relief, Sister was busy and waved her away to help with beds.

Petula's thoughts were spinning in amazement. What on earth did the man mean? Too rough? Had there been violent sex play in that seemingly innocent vehicle? And everyone was so open and cheerful about it! She saw again the vivid blue eyes gazing down at her and the soft lips that met in a kiss that may not have been textbook resuscitation, but was all she wanted to give her life.

One of the men waiting for chest surgery was watching her as she folded back the top sheet. 'I heard that you joined the fire service, Nurse.' She smiled, hoping that soon the patients would forget that old joke and she could forget the night of the fire, too.

'I decided not to take it up as a career,' she said lightly.

'There's a bit about it in the paper,' he said. 'My wife brought it in last night. I told her she was a bit late with it, but it was her neighbour who saw it and forgot to give it to her.'

He held out a torn piece of newspaper with the headline *Fire at the Princess Beatrice*. There was a photograph of the blazing balcony and one of the firemen winding out the hoses. A small picture, badly out of focus, made her stare. Angus Moray was holding a woman in his arms and emerging from the smoke like a hero in a war film.

'Take it, Nurse. I expect you'd like it. Which of the surgeons is that? We don't see him here, do we?' he said hopefully. 'And I suppose that's one of the patients.'

'He's a doctor, not a surgeon,' she said. 'And he helped us all that night.' She folded the paper and put it carefully in her pocket. It would remind her that once she had been held in those strong arms, kissed by that amazing man and desired by him, even if he never asked her for anything more than kisses.

'Thank you,' she said. 'I expect the ward sister would like to see this.' But she knew that she would keep the picture for ever, or until it was too creased and torn by folding and unfolding to be recognisable.

The bed round was finished and the dressing trolleys appeared from the clinical room. The senior staff nurse needed help and Petula was glad that something that required all her attention presented itself.

'As I go to scrub at the sink over there, Nurse, I want you to make sure the curtains are round the cubicle and be ready to let me in without contaminating my hands. You then close the curtains and take off the top sterile towel, using the forceps in the jar. I shall want you here all the time to pass me dressings and to position the patient. Now, first we go to Mr Johnston who had his operation for partial gastrectomy last week—it was an emergency. His stitches are due out today and there is a small sinus that was left to drain away the infection caused by the perforated stomach wall.

Petula braced herself to watch the dressing, wondering if it would be very traumatic. But as with everything she had encountered during her working hours on the wards, seen in the context of hospital, nothing was disturbing and she was aware only of a great need to help. Mr Johnston had such trust in the senior nurse that Petula was convinced he would accept anything suggested in the way of treatment.

'There, that wasn't too bad, was it?' The last dab of surgical spirit was applied to dry the stitch holes, and the wound sprayed. 'All the discharge has gone and you can move about more with no dressing pad. Now, Nurse Howard will hold you forward while I make sure that you breathe properly,' the staff nurse told him.

'Does Mr Johnston have physiotherapy, Nurse?' Petula asked.

'Once a day, but it's a good idea to keep the exercises going or they just slump down in bed and grumble when they get pains in their scars. We don't want that, do we?' She laughed, and Mr Johnston smiled meekly.

Petula smiled, too, amused that a man who was a person of some importance, who suffered fools badly in his own business world, should allow a girl who was no older than his daughter to dictate to him as if he was in the nursery.

The hours went quickly and when she was sent to lunch Petula realised, with surprise, that she had not thought of anything but the patients and her work all the morning. She had been kept busy emptying soiled dressing bins and bringing clean linen and dressings. She was even told to lay a tray for it as if she was used to doing it. It was another step in her career and she knew that she was growing to enjoy working with surgical cases.

Lunch was almost an intrusion, as she had been promised instruction in how to prepare a patient for the operating-theatre as soon as she went back to the ward. She hastily ate beef stew and baked potatoes and decided to miss out the pudding.

'Staff Nurse isn't back yet, Nurse Howard.' Sister glanced at the ward clock. 'You haven't taken your lunch break. I like nurses to be keen, but you have little enough free time and when you work on my ward, I expect you not only to do what you are told, but to take your full break times. The work here is hard and we haven't enough staff for you to get run down and have to go on sick leave.'

'No, Sister,' said Petula.

'But now you are here, let's lay up for the prep trolley. Put on that gown and get a mask.'

Ten minutes later, the trolley was laid with dishes of skin cleanser and antiseptic solution in spirit, to paint the skin where the incision would be made. On the lower shelf of the trolley were ordinary washing equipment and a razor and scissors to remove any hair likely to interfere with the site of operation.

'Who is for theatre, Sister Gordon?' Petula enquired.

'A man who came to us from the medical unit. We get a lot of patients referred to us when the physicians can do no more for them, or if they have been built up ready for surgery. This man, Mr Acton, has a bleeding duodenal ulcer that has not healed after drugs and rest.

He has anaemia because over a period of months he has been losing blood steadily. They did all the X-ray examinations, barium meals and blood tests in Medical, and now the surgeons will excise the affected gut. With care he will be as good as new.'

'Is he scared?' asked Petula. It sounded like a major operation.

'He's been in here in Medical for two months and he's used to us. He wants to get back to work and would go through a great deal to be well again.' Sister frowned and looked at the clock again. 'Have you seen Dr Moray? He promised to see Mr Acton before he goes to the theatre. He was under Dr Moray's team for medical treatment and so they still have an interest in his case. Stay here, Nurse, and bring him along to the bed when he arrives.'

'Yes, Sister.' Petula's mouth was dry and her hands made a creased mess of her apron as she stared at the closed swing-doors of the ward. The staff nurse came back and nodded to her but went over to the bed where Sister was talking to a patient. They drew the curtains of the cubicle and as Dr Angus Moray came into the ward, the doors swinging madly behind him, Nurse Howard was the only member of staff to greet him.

'Hello,' she said. 'Sister is over there and she said to go to see Mr Acton in the bed next to the curtains.'

'You look like death,' he said. 'How much real fresh air have you had since I saw you?'

'It's been very cold and I've been here all the time. London isn't noted for its health-giving air, is it?'

'Rubbish. You could have walked in the park or something. Fed the ducks in St James's, for example.' He shrugged, as if shrugging off all responsibility for her.

Sister came towards them. 'Ah, there you are, Dr Moray. How nice of you to give up your time to come back.' She beamed at him and Petula wondered if any woman was immune to his charm.

'I keep my promises, Sister Gordon.' He gave her a dazzling smile that Petula couldn't help contrasting with the cold look of professional appraisal *she* had been given when he came into the ward. He turned to her as she stood wondering if she could escape. 'What have you been doing to my nurse, Sister?'

'She *does* look peaky.' They regarded Petula with interest. 'I think she is your department. If you must let your nurses get carbon monoxide poisoning, what can you expect?' Sister Gordon sounded as if she knew the handsome doctor very well. Not another willing victim? But Sister Gordon was wide-hipped and motherly and by no stretch of the imagination could she be thought of as a paramour.

'I had to bring Delia back for duty and I thought I could see Mr Acton as I promised, but if there is anything more you need, Sister, I'm not here! I have to get back and finish my week of leave.'

'All alone? You need someone with you, surely?'

'Delia was a disappointment. She thought she had more free time—and now I find that even my house physician isn't quite convinced that she could put up with me!'

Sister smiled in such a way that Petula felt shocked. 'I can't see any of the staff refusing to go with you, Dr Moray. The sooner you see your patient, the sooner you can be off again.' She walked away, chuckling, to speak to the girl with the reports from the Medical Records Department.

'So, Sister has deserted me, Nurse Howard. Do you think you have enough energy to help me?' Petula blushed, aware of his close scrutiny and cross with her own reaction to his nearness. He smiled bleakly. 'You look as if you've seen a ghost. You aren't going to pass out on me again, are you?'

'No, I'm perfectly all right,' she said. 'Shall I get the notes for Mr Acton?' He nodded and she knew that he watched her as she went into the office.

'The notes? That's right, Nurse. You can cope with Mr Acton. Just make sure that you ask Dr Moray to speak to me before he leaves. I want to know a few details about the diet and I was hoping that he would tell us his opinion of Mr Acton's temperament—some people have a tendency to worry far too much. In the case of gastrics, this can hold up their recovery. If Dr Moray thinks it necessary we might have to prescribe a mild tranquiliser for the post-operative period. If Mr Acton continues to pour out acid on the unaffected part of his duodenum, he could have another ulcer,' Sister explained.

'Do I take the X-rays, too, Sister?'

'No, we don't use the ward viewer any more. Some of the patients see them and think that they are looking at their own X-rays. One man swore that he had an ulcer after seeing X-rays in the ward viewer that a house surgeon had left after an examination.' Sister smiled dryly. 'He was in for a hernia! Some people think they have one cavity in the body where everything mixes up and he had no idea where a gastric ulcer would be on the plate. We do have a viewer in the small side ward, and a table that the doctors can use for notes. They can talk in there to students, without being heard by the patients.'

'Yes, Sister.' Petula half hoped that Sister would take over, but she was dismissed with a nod. The notes were quite bulky as Mr Acton had attended Outpatients for years for one complaint after another. Now he was hoping to be free from pain for the first time for ages.

'I have the notes, Dr Moray,' she said, and stood by the small opening in the curtains of the cubicle.

'Bring them in, Nurse. Did Sister tell you to stay?'

'Yes.' She bit back the words she had planned. She was about to suggest that he didn't need her and could she be excused, but now that she knew that Sister had told her to stay with him she had no escape.

'Good,' he said, briskly. 'I want to go over his chest.' He looked down at the pale-faced man. 'We are old friends, Mr Acton! A pity that diet wasn't enough, but I'm sure the surgeons will help you a great deal.'

He held out his hand and Petula put the notes into it. 'Not that, Nurse. I will read the reports later. I probably know most of that by heart.' He twitched his fingers, as if wanting some other paper or instrument to be put into his hand.

'I don't know what you want, Dr Moray.'

'You don't?' A slow smile mocked her and she wondered if he was thinking of her as she had been when the iron stairway tore her uniform dress from her on the night of the fire. Even Mr Acton managed a wintry smile, sensing the mildly sensual exchange between the pretty nurse and the tall dark Scot.

'If you want the X-rays, Sister said the viewer is in the side ward. And if you need a stethoscope, I'll have to get one from Sister's office.'

He patted his pocket and looked quite surprised to find a stethoscope in the depths of the white coat.

'I didn't know I brought one. Oh, it belongs to Ward Nine.'

He looked as if he had no part in its being in his pocket and Petula wondered just how often irate sisters had to chase equipment that he had absent-mindedly taken.

'I have one of my own, somewhere, but I

never seem to be able to find it.' He stuck the ear-pieces in place and motioned to Petula to undo the pyjama jacket of the man on the bed.

She watched the serious concentration as firm hands and the shiny metal drum explored and probed the chest wall to make sure that the patient was fit to receive an anaesthetic. The doctor's auburn hair was almost tidy, with a tendency to wave in a casual and attractive manner and the blue eyes held an expression of caring. As he looked down at the worried man, his smile was warm and comforting.

'Now the back, Nurse.' Petula held the man forward, resting his head on her shoulder to expose the back and to expand the muscles. Mr Acton seemed far too thin and light for a man of five feet eleven, and she wanted to tell him that he would soon be better.

She sensed the doctor at her side, his shoulder touching hers as he bent over the patient. He smelled of the same soap or aftershave as she remembered when he had kissed her in the duty room of the medical ward. His face was close to hers and he grinned as he removed the stethoscope from his ears and rested the ear-pieces round his neck.

'No, stay there, Nurse,' he said, and palpated the chest wall carefully as Petula held the patient.

He was very close to her. She had no option but to stay with her face over the patient's shoulder, his head turned away from her as he rested comfortably in the examination position. There was nothing she could do unless she dropped a patient who was due for surgery the following day, and as Dr Angus Moray came closer still and pressed his cool, firm mouth to hers, she could only submit while he took his time over a lingering and deepening kiss. He stopped her when she drew back.

'I haven't finished, Nurse,' he said, cooly.

'I have to change my position, Doctor. I'm getting cramp,' she said in a loud voice. In another moment, I shall shake like a leaf, she thought, and Mr Acton will think I'm completely mad. I must be mad! This can't be happening! But Dr Moray was putting the stethoscope away as if he had nothing on his mind other than the welfare of his patient.

'Interesting,' he said. 'I had some very interesting reactions to that examination. You are very fit, Mr Acton, and should have no trouble tomorrow.' He smiled kindly. 'But I think I took too long. Poor Nurse Howard isn't very strong and I think it was a strain for her to hold you.' He watched her button the pyjama jacket. 'Oh, dear, you'll have to start again. You missed one buttonhole, Nurse. That's better.'

Petula fumed inwardly. How dared he treat her like that, just for his own amusement? How could he tease her, knowing that he had gone too far and been thoroughly unethical? But there had been no other person involved and certainly nothing had been done to hurt a patient, so she couldn't really accuse him of that.

To be honest, if it had happened with any of

the other doctors or house surgeons, she could have dismissed it as a bit of cheeky fun. But her feelings for Angus were so profound that she could find no excuse for him, even if he had no lasting and deep love for her.

'The X-rays, Nurse?' She tried to hate the bland and amused voice, but could only wonder at the blue of his eyes and the soft memory of his lips on hers. She tucked in the sheet and pulled the bed-table closer. 'You can pull back the curtains, Nurse. I shall have no further need for . . . privacy.'

You devil! she wanted to say. How could I love you?

'The X-rays are in the side ward. You don't need me now, do you?' was all that she uttered.

'Of course I do.' He sounded surprised. 'You can study them and learn something. I think that some of your knowledge has serious gaps. It is my duty to fill in and to help.' She glanced at him. His lips were still, his eyes calm and his manner perfect. Once more, she couldn't believe that it had happened.

Was this how he behaved with Sister Tyley? Did he make love to her and then switch his attention to other matters and expect her to accept the sudden change in manner? What woman would be able to take such treatment?

But she was beginning to know the answer to that. If you called, I would come, she thought. Smile that gentle smile and I am your slave. Take me in your arms and hold me close and I am yours for ever.

It was an impossible situation and she ached to get away and to find something or someone to take his place—even if it was only in a superficial way. She followed slowly, carrying the notes and the stethoscope that he had once more left behind as he finished with the patient.

The X-rays were neatly stacked and Petula found the ones needed. She spread them out on the table and switched on the bright light behind the viewer. She could feel Angus Moray behind her and strove to ignore him. He took an X-ray, slid it under the clips at the side of the viewer and stared at it.

'Do you see?' He pointed to the dark irregularity where the barium meal was opaque to X-ray and filled the depression caused by the ulcer. He put another plate beside the first. 'This was taken after the first you saw. He has had dietary treatment for six weeks and we found that he was responding to one particular anti-acid preparation in which there was a lot of magnesium trisilicate. But then he had a lot of worries at home, and when he came to Outpatients he was in pain again.'

He added another. 'This is as good as we could manage on diet alone. He is a born worrier and the sooner we operate, the sooner he will get back to work and know that life holds something for him again.'

'Wouldn't it have been easier to have operated in the first place?' Petula asked quietly.

He looked down at her, smiling that mocking but gentle smile. 'And do us poor physicians out of a job?' He laughed. 'Don't look like that! I can see that you take everything you are told as gospel truth. Relax, Nurse Howard, life can be fun if you give a little.'

She backed away from him. 'And now your adrenalin is working overtime and you want to run away,' he said.

'No,' she replied, without conviction.

He placed a hand on each of her shoulders and she saw just how tall he was, how wide-shouldered and how his fingers pressed into her soft flesh. He regarded her in silence, his eyes seeming to search hers for some message. She had to look up and meet the brightness and the question, but she could do nothing but breathe deeply and hope that she didn't disgrace herself by flinging herself deeper into his arms. It was too much to be held in that way and to have her face exposed to his searching gaze. He bent to kiss her softly and she shivered and then drew away. He let his hands fall to his sides, and when Sister came into the side ward he was studying the last of the X-rays.

'Ah, there you are, Doctor. Everything in order?' Petula saw his glance wander over her legs and body and then back to the X-rays.

'Fine, Sister. Mr Acton has nothing wrong with his chest and I am convinced that surgery is the only course left if he is to recover fully.'

'You have spent a lot of time with him. I wish that all the men were as devoted.'

'I am very devoted, Sister,' he said solemnly, and Petula stood back so that the conversation couldn't possibly include her.

'And now you can go back and finish your leave.'

'So I can.' He sounded sad. 'But I shall now be alone. It seems such a waste, doesn't it?'

'You should have someone to keep you company. Nurse Howard looks pale, as if she needs a little stimulation. Why not take her?'

Petula looked from one to the other. I *am* here, she wanted to say. I know I'm small and pale and insignificant enough to be picked up and put down as soon as I'm not wanted, but you are talking about me as if I was a fly on the wall!

'You are quite right, Sister.' He smiled sweetly. 'I get lost easily and I need someone to hold my hand.'

Sister Gordon turned to the nurse. 'You are off this evening, I believe.' Petula nodded, a feeling of impending nemesis threatening her. 'And this is your weekend off, too? I had a note from Admin suggesting a break after a day or so on duty.'

'Yes, I am off duty, Sister, but I could stay. I feel fine now,' she said, too eagerly.

'She's off duty and feels fine, so I think you have a passenger, Doctor. That is, unless you have a date with your boyfriend, Nurse Howard?' Sister looked as if this would be quite unreasonable and Petula couldn't force herself to lie.

'I have no plans, Sister, but I have a lot of studying to do,' she said desperately.

'I hesitate to ask her,' Angus Moray said. They were doing it again!

'I *am* here, Dr Moray,' Petula flared, risking being told off for impertinence to a senior member of the medical staff and the ward sister.

'So you are, but to look at you, you could slip out under the door.' He grinned. 'I prescribe fresh air and a change of scene. I take it I have your full co-operation, Sister?'

'I couldn't agree more, and you'll probably enjoy the weekend once you know what's expected of you.'

'I want to stay here and read,' Petula said angrily. 'I don't want fresh air.' She was appalled. The permissive society was one thing, but open discussion of what could only be a dirty weekend was too much!

'I think it would do you a lot of good, Nurse. Come back on Monday and tell me all about it.'

Petula turned to Angus Moray, her eyes bright with the hurt she felt. 'And what if I don't want to be one of your birds?'

She leaned on the table for support. The gust of laughter that greeted her words could, she imagined, be heard at the other end of the ward. She glared at the two professional people who were laughing at her.

'Now what have I said?'

Angus sobered first. 'I'm sorry,' he said, and a curiously tender expression made Petula blush. 'You didn't know? Oh, dear, this is awful, Sister. I really don't think that Nurse Howard knows what I do on these trips!'

Sister was pink-cheeked. 'Oh, dear, what

you must think, Nurse? Sort it out between you while I give Mr Acton his medicine.' She went away, muttering and laughing.

'Stop teasing me,' said Petula with tears in her eyes. 'I am so very confused.'

'Sit there,' he said and she sank into the one deep chair by the table. He loomed above her. 'You see,' he began, gently, 'one of my main hobbies, or obsessions, if you like, is bird-watching. I go to the east coast and help with the charting of migratory birds, cleaning off oil and ringing them for future research. At this time of the year, there are many on the Norfolk coastline, all needing more help than I have time to give, so I take a van and bully anyone off duty into coming with me to help whenever I get the opportunity. I've equipped the van with everything we need, and we use it as a hide, too, if the weather is bad. We can watch and count birds in comfort rather than lying on boggy ice and getting pneumonia.'

She hung her head, feeling an idiot. 'I'm sorry, but how was I to know?'

'I'm the one to apologise,' he said. 'Will you come? I promise it won't be arduous. I have to write up the count I did yesterday and I hope to spot some Bewick swans.'

'I know nothing about birds,' she protested feebly.

'You can write down what I see and help when I need four hands.' He looked serious. 'It is work that is crying out to be done and I need all the help I can get.' He smiled. 'Bring plenty of warm clothes and some wellies if you have them, and I give you my word that you will not suffer in any way.' He looked down at her, his eyes twinkling. 'Don't be afraid. I won't capture you unless you want to be my prisoner.'

She blushed and looked away, afraid he could read her thoughts and unable to bear this new friendliness. He was giving her an option and she would be safe with him. It mattered more to him now that she went as a helper than if she was willing for him to make love to her. He wanted her, physically, but not as much as he wanted a nurse or an assistant. She could go as a helper and as a friend or lover—the choice would be hers.

Petula looked up and sounded quite calm. 'I'll come,' she said, and knew that she was completely mad. Would she have any choice if she was with him for hours, touching him, seeing him, listening to his voice and watching his profile while he looked at the sky? He looked delighted and complacent as if he had got exactly what he wanted. And the nights? What of the nights alone with him in a confined space in the depths of a marsh, where each sound would be unfriendly to a girl not used to such forays?

She put out a hand to stop him but he turned away and strode from the room. She had to tell him that it was impossible and she wanted out. It was bad enough seeing him in a professional context, when the slightest touch of his hand on hers made her thrill with uncontrollable bliss, and she couldn't believe that he would leave her completely alone if she went with him. I'll just have to wear layers and layers of unattractive clothing and make myself look as revolting as possible, she thought gloomily.

CHAPTER EIGHT

THERE WAS no excuse left for Nurse Petula
Howard to stay on duty. The clinical room was
tidy and she had done quite a lot to help the
next shift when they had to cope with evening
treatments and dressings. Dr Angus Moray
popped his head round the door and smiled.
'Don't forget. I'll pick you up at seven.'

'Tonight?' She stared at him in horror. 'But
we can't count birds in the dark!'

He laughed. 'We can amuse ourselves
tonight and make our plans for the morning.
Don't be late.' He came back and she was
standing frozen with bewilderment. 'And
bring a pretty dress. We shall eat at the hotel,'
he said.

Camper-van, hotel, bird-watching? Travel-
ling to the east coast and arriving after every
self-respecting bird had roosted for the night?
It was surely the weakest explanation she had
heard. Did Sister really know what went on
during these weekends? Petula's brain seemed
unable to function and she knew there was no
backing away from this one. She had promised
to go and it would seem very odd if she didn't
turn up when he called for her.

Sister was too helpful. 'You can go off duty
now, Nurse. You've done very well for the first
time back and I know that when you come here

after the break you will fit in just fine.'

'I felt better as soon as I started work again, Sister. I can stay if you are going to be busy tomorrow. It seems hardly fair to go off now after such a short time on duty,' Petula suggested.

'I wouldn't dream of depriving you of your weekend. I'm sure that Dr Moray will take great care of you and I think you are a very lucky girl. Most of the nurses here would give a lot to go away with such a handsome man.'

She glanced shrewdly at the pale face. 'It will buck you up no end to have a good-looking man dancing attendance on you.'

'I think I'm the one who will be doing the fetching and carrying,' said Petula lightly. 'He probably works his helpers to death. He can be very unreasonable when he is engrossed in something that interests him.' She laughed bravely. 'I'll take a couple of paperbacks to read if I find it boring.'

Brave words, she thought, when she was safely off duty and Sister could no longer go on and on about the wonderful man and raking up little incidents to prove her point. I've enough to think about without being told what I already know and feel with every fibre of my being, she thought. Dulcie wasn't much help, either. She burst into the bedroom and saw the half-packed, squashy bag lying on a chair.

'Not running away, surely?' she asked.

'No, you idiot. I'm off for the weekend.'

'You didn't say you'd be going down to Tunbridge.' Dulcie reached for Petula's writing-paper. 'Could you take a note for David? I can write it here in five minutes.'

'I'm not going to Tunbridge, Dulcie. Wait for it! I'm going bird-watching,' Petula announced.

'You're doing *what*? I didn't think you knew a robin from a thrush.' Dulcie looked startled.

'I don't. I hate birds and I hate being cold. I am completely nuts to be conned into this situation and I want to run away,' her friend raised her hands in despair.

'Tell me more.' Dulcie was laughing at the woebegone expression. 'Is this some kind of joke?'

'No, I am going to count birds—and unless I am very careful, I may even have to ring them. Before the weekend is over, I shall be an authority on the great northern diver, all kinds of auk, oily guillemots *and* the greater bear, Dr Bird-watcher Moray.'

'Have you flipped your lid?'

'I told you—and to be honest, Dulcie, I am busily telling me, too—I just don't believe it! I am going with Angus Moray in that sinister camper-van to save birds from an oily death.' Petula grimaced, trying to make light of her fears.

'Stop it, Pet!' Dulcie sat back on the bed and laughed. 'You really are the end. You, bird-watching in that cosy passion waggon? Save the birds, you say? Who is going to save *you*?' She giggled helplessly. 'I've heard some excuses for a romantic weekend, but that beats the lot!'

'It's true! Ask Sister Tyley or Dr Arran. They've been with him on similar weekends, sometimes with other people with more vehicles, and sometimes alone.' Petula gave a hollow laugh. 'Lou Sheridan went once, but that hardly gives a ring of respectability, does it? I expect he thought it might be more exciting than it was. Now I know that Dr Angus Moray has a hobby—birds.'

'I'll bet it is. My godfathers! All alone on the blasted heath or wherever, with the most incredible man, next to David, that I know. Petula, you are either the most gullible twit in history or you are very, very cunning. A night or two alone with him and I think you could have him for good. I've seen the way he looks at you.'

'For heaven's sake stop, Dulcie! He doesn't want me. He fancies me a bit, but only second to whatever happens to interest him more. Sometimes I think he dislikes me. He told me today that I looked like death. I'm going bird-watching with him and when we come back on Sunday night, I'm afraid you will be very disappointed. I shall have taken a few notes, watched a few bedraggled birds and caught up on my paperbacks—and he will be bored to tears with me for knowing so little. You heard how he carried on in the lecture room and he gave me another lecture in the ward. He can't forget his work for one minute.'

'Take a warm nightie,' teased Dulcie. 'Is it double sleeping-bags or single bunks?'

'I hate you,' said Petula, blushing furiously.

'I shall come back and ask Andy to marry me and then you'll have to take back all the unkind things you've said.' She laughed with a tremor in her voice. 'Don't make it worse, Dulcie, I really am scared.'

'You needn't be scared. Angus is great and I know he wouldn't hurt a hair of your head—or even a tiny feather. Pack loads of warm things. Where's that lovely hat and scarf set you had for Christmas? It certainly looks good. Or I have a very thick woolly set that you can borrow with pleasure,' Dulcie offered.

'No, I don't want to dress up. What I mean is, I must wear old clothes so it doesn't matter when they get dirty.'

'It's no use you trying to hide behind beige tweed, Petula. Angus knows there's more to you than that.'

Petula blushed again, knowing that he had once seen more of her body than she wanted exposed. At least she wouldn't have to strip off in a bleak estuary.

Eventually she had everything she thought she might need, including a heavy waterproof cape that was fine for fell-walking and doubled as a cover and a ground sheet. Enough to rob the most beautiful woman of glamour, Petula thought with satisfaction, and she brought out a bright orange anorak that did nothing for her, either.

She hesitated before the rack of clothes in her wardrobe. She had to take something good to wear in the hotel for dinner, and the dress she chose was softly blue and draped sleekly over her hips to fall in a wide, sighing skirt of silk. Her pale grey suede shoes matched the sheer tights and handbag and the short matching jacket would be a warm enough cover if she wore the clothes in the hotel and not in the cold outside air.

She frowned as she finished packing. It wasn't ideal to change for dinner in the hotel cloakroom and then back into her thick casuals for a night in the van, but she was in Angus's hands as far as practical arrangements went. If only she could make sure during dinner that he knew her resolution to avoid playing a fast game with him, all might be well and they could settle down to enjoying a friendly time together. She caught a glimpse of her face in the mirror and thought she looked like a belligerent commando under the unbecoming knitted hat, her hair stuffed safely inside it.

Just as well, she thought, morosely. But when she met Angus at the car park, she looked small and vulnerable under the mass of wool, and the elfin shape of her face was doubly poignant when he looked down at her.

'Very nice,' he said, dryly. 'Where on earth did you find that hat?'

'Don't you like it?' She smiled wickedly, believing that she looked very unappetising. He grunted and shifted a case further into the van, pushing her own grip after it. She peeped inside. It looked a bit spartan and at the back was a large metal tank under two slung bunks. A double-bottle gas cooker stood by a small sink and a single seat ran along one side of the vehicle.

'Good, isn't it?' he said, with pride. 'I stripped it down to essentials and it's very convenient.'

'Nice,' she said, and huddled into her jacket. In one way she was reassured. This van could never be the passion-waggon that Dulcie hinted it might be. But she was also disappointed. It looked so utilitarian that she might have misjudged him entirely once more.

Was he a bird fanatic who would work his helper hard just to get his data? Would he have any time to notice that Nurse Howard was pretty and nubile? Far from fighting off the advances of a known lecher, she might even have to beg him to notice that she was hungry!

'Up in front with me,' he said. 'I rang through to make sure we have dinner.' Petula stepped up into the cab and found it warm and comfortable. So far, so good. The roads were not busy as soon as they left town and the powerful engine made the journey enjoyable and easy. They sped past towns on bypasses and motorways and all the time they travelled, Angus talked as if he was completely relaxed in her company. His admiration for the Princess Beatrice was apparent and Petula felt a warm glow that she was now a part of the centre of healing.

'Apart from the bad bits, what did you think of the allergy ward?' he enquired.

'It's a very good idea, but surely you need to do it on a full time basis with regular staff and follow-ups like they have for the diabetic wing?' Petula glanced up at him, wondering if he might resent the views of a very junior nurse, but he urged her to go on and tell him the reactions of the patients involved in the tests.

'They loved the extra attention,' she said, 'but Nurse Bolton wondered if they might react to the tests in a different way in their own surroundings. One of the women said that she felt fine when she was in bed in the ward with no worries, but at home she had a family and a job in a supermarket where she is kept very busy all day.'

'And she was worse at home?'

'She said she could feel the build-up of acids as she got more and more hot and overworked, and when she reached home, she ate handfuls of sodium bicarbonate tablets to take away the discomfort.'

He laughed. 'I can just imagine how she felt. We ask for volunteers among the students to sit in bed for two days and have different potions put down Ryle's tubes, then test as we did the ones in the balcony ward. The poor blighter who was fed dilute hydrochloric acid, as found in excess acidity, said that he will have the greatest interest and sympathy with all the gastrics he meets when he is in a medical ward. Anyone with a stomach ache will get VIP treatment from him!'

'Do you make use of everyone you meet?' Petula asked. He used the sisters to get extra beds for his cases, he used students to help in his tests and he used staff to go with him on some crazy outing to count birds! And she suspected that he must use his own powerful sensuality to get what he needed as and when he wanted sex. She knew that she had been mad to come with him.

'We all use people in various ways,' he said quietly.

'We don't all make people do what they would rather not do.'

'There is a certain expertise in choosing those who are willing victims, even if they don't realise that they might enjoy what is suggested when it is first mentioned.'

Petula blushed and sank down in her seat. Was this a warm-up for something other than ringing birds? She knew her own weakness and now he knew that she would be a willing victim. She would do exactly as he wanted, if it was washing filthy birds or holding fluttering creatures while he ringed them. If it came to him wanting her in any other way, she would be lost in her own deep emotions.

'How far now?' She was more tired than she had thought. The events of the day had taken more of her reserves than she knew and she no longer worried about this first night. I shall fall asleep and be of no use for anything, as soon as I have eaten, she thought. She looked back at the slung bunks and smiled. Not the best place for a seduction scene with a weary girl.

'Nearly there. I know the way and we shall be there in five minutes. Hungry?' She nodded. 'Good. They serve very satisfying meals. A lot of bird-watchers stay there and we can have packed lunches and get water and gas there.'

The van was very basic and as he spoke of the hotel it sounded rather like a youth hostel, serving thick sandwiches and vegetable stew. The thought of the pretty dress in her grip made her wonder if the other guests would sit down to eat in their wellies and fishing hats.

But as she entered the softly-lit hall of the country hotel, she gasped with pleasure. Early daffodils in huge copper vases made pools of glowing colour in corners, and a log fire burned in each of the two lounges. 'Drink first, or change?' he asked.

'I'm much too hot in this,' she said.

'I'd rather change first,' he agreed. 'Then we can settle down for the night.' He took her grip and walked to the lift, with two keys in his other hand.

'Where do I change?'

'In your room, of course. You didn't think we slept in the van, did you?'

'Er . . . no, of course not,' she said, and hurried after him.

'Meet you in fifteen minutes, or I die of hunger,' he said and left her at the open door of a pretty room, wondering if she was dreaming. So they didn't spend intimate nights alone on the river bank or the sea shore!

Petula laughed, and the relief was overwhelming. As she changed, her colour rose and bloomed more naturally than at any time since Christmas. It didn't matter. Nothing mattered tonight. She could face the working day in the somewhat bleak van, but here she had a room to herself, a warm and delightful room where she could lock the door and sleep.

A tap on the door made her start. She took a last look at her reflection and went out to Angus, who put a hand out to take her room key. He put it in the pocket of the blue velvet jacket with his own and smiled at her with approval.

On any other man his clothes might seem ordinary and casual, but the blue matched the soft azure of his eyes and the leonine head was held proudly, as if he was indeed the king of his pride. The pale silk shirt was immaculate and the sober blue tie had more impact than an elaborate one would have had.

He eyed her quizzically. 'Is it the same girl?' She fluttered her eyelashes in confusion. 'I had a feeling that you couldn't have put on all that weight since I last saw you.'

'I was cold,' she said defensively. She tossed her head and the well-brushed hair rippled over her face to hide her blushes. 'You look different too,' she said, as if accusing him of disguise.

'Two new people. That's a very satisfactory situation. A good beginning. We are here together, away from work and friends. Here we can decide if we like what we find out about each other and, perhaps more important, about ourselves.'

'I know about me,' she said.

'I doubt it,' he said with a familiar tinge

of arrogance. 'Gin and tonic or a Bloody Mary?'

'Just a small sherry,' she said.

He ordered and took the menu from the bar while the barman rang through for a waiter to come for the order.

'There's quite a good choice,' he said.

Petula laughed. 'It's not a bit as I thought it would be. I thought it would be very stodgy, with everyone talking about the lesser red-shank or something.'

'Life is full of surprises,' he said. 'You might even discover that I hardly ever bite.' She looked round the bar at the other guests. He couldn't do anything here but be charming and encourage her to order and to eat a good meal. Their table was by a heavily curtained window and Petula pulled aside one of the drapes to look out. She drew back sharply as the chill came through the glass.

'I'm glad I don't have to go outside tonight,' she said. 'It looks as if it could turn to snow.'

He leaned over and his shoulder touched her breast. A pain that was all sweetness engulfed her and her new-found confidence and bravado were shattered. How could she bear to be with him alone, away from the gently-lit hotel and the bars and lounges that were never free of people? If she prayed very hard, could it be too cold to go out tomorrow?

'Ready for an early start tomorrow?' She looked blank. 'I like to be there by seven.'

'It's pitch black at seven!'

'That's right. The birds are still asleep and

we can get into position with binoculars and watch the dawn come up over the marsh. It's very satisfying. It's like being on another planet.'

'It sounds horrible. I thought that this was a part of my convalescence?'

'So it is. Plenty of good food, which I saw that you ate with a very good appetite, and tonight you sleep in a cosy bed, with every comfort. Tomorrow, the treatment includes lots of fresh air and exercise. I really am doing you a favour, Nurse Howard.'

He laughed and she was forced to smile. 'Be ready at six-thirty for breakfast. Your room or mine?' She glanced at him sharply and then knew that he was laughing at her.

'I'll come down here,' she said, primly.

'If you aren't ready, I'll haul you out of bed.'

'I'll be dressed and down here,' she said hastily.

'And so to bed.' He smiled down at her as they came to the door of her room. His eyes were gentle. 'Sleep well, Petula.'

'Goodnight,' she said, and put out her hand for the key. He handed it to her and inclined his head, without another word.

She stepped into her room and closed the door. He had gone without a goodnight kiss or even a touch. He had handed over the key as if to make any contact with her would burn his fingers. All the defences that she had built up during the evening, all the efforts to be free of tension, were for nothing. She had expected some form of confrontation, even if it was only a half-derisive and teasing kiss to make her know that, if he really wanted her, he could take her with her full consent.

She was hot with a kind of shame. It was a relief but also a blow to her pride. He had left her at her door, his only concern being that she was ready in time to watch some wretched, squawking birds climb out of their soggy nests at some ungodly hour before sane people were awake.

As she tossed in angry wakefulness, she found him impossible to understand. One half of her mind told her that he wanted her as much as she wanted him, and the other half was afraid that she had passed on the message far too skilfully. Perhaps he really thought she was immune to his charm and had no intention of satisfying his sexual needs.

Petula tugged at her pillow. How could she ever live it down in her own mind? To be alone with a man as masculine and virile as Angus Moray and to be left completely alone! I'll never get to sleep, she thought distractedly, and promptly fell into a deep slumber in which strange, disjointed images appeared and made her toss and turn.

The small alarm which she took with her when she was away from home gave her a shock when she opened one eye and discovered that the outside world was dark. She stared at the black sky in horror and disbelief. The man was insane and heartless! The birds wouldn't thank him for waking them up, she thought sourly. Who wanted humans to see the first bedraggled stretching of the day? Then she had a sudden panic and threw on layers of clothes in case his tap came on her door before she was dressed. She picked up her holdall and books and breathed slowly to compose her mind. Ah well, she would survive, and if she was thoroughly cross and bored when the weekend was over, at least she could brush him from her life and love and thoughts. Which is what I have to do, she decided.

He was waiting, dressed very much as she was, but she wished that he could look less masculine and rugged, less completely efficient, cheerful, and . . . wonderful. He thrust a wicker basket in her direction.

'That's lunch,' he said. 'Put it in the van.' He followed with a pile of blankets and a large electric lantern.

'Is it going to be *that* dark?' He put it in the van with enough equipment to last them a week.

'I like to be prepared,' he said.

'Sounds like a lovely picnic,' she said dryly.

'Doesn't it just?' he replied with enthusiasm. 'Come on, or we'll miss the best bit.'

'I could bear it,' she muttered, but he was too busy stowing things neatly and didn't hear her.

The darkness had an edge of grey, slowly changing to silver. The reluctant dawn was painfully red and the sky clear and frosty. The wheels of the van crunched ice as it fought a way through rutted mud and beaten sedge, and in spite of her dislike of early mornings,

Petula leaned forward and knew something of the excitement of an explorer finding fresh new lands. They reached a dip by an estuary with a wide view of the skyline and Angus stopped the engine. The heater was switched on in the back of the van and the curtains were drawn so that they could watch the water while sitting in comfort.

Angus took down one of the bunks to make a seat and piled blankets on it to make sure that Petula was raised high enough to see everything. It was all done without reference to her but she knew that all the effort was for her benefit and was oddly touched that he should bother. He handed her a pair of binoculars and pointed to a clump of rushes. She focussed and gave a gasp as a skein of geese rose like silent ghosts from the reed bed and scoured the sky, their wings making music as they beat the air, breaking the silence. She scanned the water as more and more birds came into view.

'Coffee?' he said, and she put the glasses down.

'Oh, shouldn't I be doing that? I thought that was my job.'

'So did I, but with those things glued to your eyes, I hadn't the heart to disturb you.' He was smiling and the warm radiance growing with the daylight touched his hair where it tumbled on his brow.

'I had no idea that it could be so beautiful,' she said, and put out a hand for the mug of coffee. 'Thank you,' she said softly, looking away from the gaze that threatened her with its intensity.

He sat close to her on the blankets and she had to break the silence. 'I always believed that bird-watchers were dim or lazy. I know nothing about birds,' she said, with growing humility.

'I'm glad you like it, Petula.' He sipped his coffee, watching her over the rim of the mug. 'I can teach you, if you want me to.' She nodded. 'I find this place relaxing and I can think and be objective here. Have you ever had problems that seem completely without an answer? Sometimes believing that what you want to do will never be sorted out?'

'Very often,' she said. 'But I can never think of you being at a loss.'

'Surely you know the tensions within our professions, even if you have been at Beatties for less than five minutes,' he said, smiling in the teasing way that she half resented.

'You are so sure of your own abilities—and, of course, you are nearly always right,' she said. 'The patients think you are God.' She glanced sideways to see his reaction.

He laughed. 'Only one of the lesser Greek variety, I'm afraid, and we all know what mistakes they made. I need all the confidence I can muster at times.'

'That's not the impression you give. Frankly, I can't believe it. I have never seen you at a disadvantage and you've no idea how depressing it is to be slapped down by a paragon who does no wrong.'

'I never do that!' Petula laughed aloud and he went slightly red. 'Well, hardly ever. It's just that I know what I want and I go after it—perhaps too eagerly.' He paused and she held her breath, wondering what he was about to say. 'I *do* know what I want, Nurse Howard, and there are times when I am so worried that I can hardly think.'

'You, worried? About a case?'

'I remember a case that worried me sick.' He looked out as if to see beyond the rising dawn. 'I had a waking nightmare. I was trying to get to a patient through a bolted door and I knew that she was in grave danger.'

Petula sat wide-eyed and very still, wondering at the pain in the deep blue eyes. She could feel the colour ebbing from her cheeks and hardly dared to breathe.

'I was frantic,' he went on. 'I ran to another entrance, only to find her lying on the floor as if dead. I took her in my arms and she was warm and lovely and I knew, even then, when I wasn't sure that she would live, that I loved her and wanted her as I had wanted no other person in my whole life.'

He turned to her and rescued the thick mug from her hands. His eyes were full of the memory of that night and the deep hurt in a man's soul. 'Petula, my darling, if you had died, I would have gone mad.'

She was in his arms, a bulky bundle of self-preservation that suddenly wanted to throw off the fetters of clothes and the restrictions of convention. He loved her, and she didn't care if they were snowed up for a week! He loved her and who cared if they counted birds?

'Angus!' was all she could say. He kissed her lips and her eyes and then tore off the ugly hat to run his fingers through her hair. His cheeks were smooth as she remembered them in the smoke and his arms were safety and danger, a haven and a thrilling challenge.

She surfaced for breath. 'But last night you were so cold,' she said. 'You didn't even kiss me when I went to bed.'

He took her hands and kissed the small wrists. He put her hands lightly on his shoulders and then took her face. His eyes spoke to her of wonders that were almost too bright.

'If I had kissed you then, I could not have gone to a lonely bed.'

'And now?' she breathed.

'It is a very cold dawn and you are dressed as if to repell an army.' She blushed, knowing he could read her mind. 'And we have work to do. But not yet.'

He held her close. Dawn brought bright sunlight and men fishing in the river. Two walkers over the marsh shouted and disturbed the birds. Petula stirred in his arms.

'I thought you had to ring some birds?'

'The men out there have disturbed them. Later, we may find some.' He went to his pack and found a small box. 'Will this do, unless you hate the stones?'

She opened it and saw three sapphires wink-

ing up at her from a base of diamonds. 'You
knew!'

'I hoped,' he said, simply. 'The ring belonged to my grandmother and I loved her
very much. She would have liked you.'

He smiled. 'Let me put it on. It is my right,
and I can't go back to Beatties and confess that
I wasted a full dawn without ringing a single
bird.'

Mills & Boon

4 Doctor Nurse Romances
FREE

Coping with the daily tragedies and ordeals of a busy hospital, and sharing the satisfaction of a difficult job well done, people find themselves unexpectedly drawn together. Mills & Boon Doctor Nurse Romances capture perfectly the excitement, the intrigue and the emotions of modern medicine, that so often lead to overwhelming and blissful love. By becoming a regular reader of Mills & Boon Doctor Nurse Romances you can enjoy EIGHT superb new titles every two months plus a whole range of special benefits: your very own personal membership card, a free newsletter packed with recipes, competitions, bargain book offers, plus big cash savings.

AND an Introductory FREE GIFT for YOU.
Turn over the page for details.

**Fill in and send this coupon back today
and we'll send you**

4 Introductory
Doctor Nurse Romances yours to keep
FREE

At the same time we will reserve a
subscription to Mills & Boon
Doctor Nurse Romances for you. Every
two months you will receive the latest
8 new titles, delivered direct to your door.
You don't pay extra for delivery. Postage and
packing is always completely Free.
There is no obligation or commitment –
you receive books only for
as long as you want to.

**It's easy! Fill in the coupon below and return it to
MILLS & BOON READER SERVICE, FREEPOST, P.O. BOX 236,
CROYDON, SURREY CR9 9EL.**

**Please note: READERS IN SOUTH AFRICA write to
Mills & Boon Ltd., Postbag X3010,
Randburg 2125, S. Africa.**

- - - - - - - - - - - - - - - - - - - -

FREE BOOKS CERTIFICATE

**To: Mills & Boon Reader Service, FREEPOST, P.O. Box 236,
Croydon, Surrey CR9 9EL.**

Please send me, free and without obligation, four Dr. Nurse Romances, and reserve a
Reader Service Subscription for me. If I decide to subscribe I shall receive, following my free
parcel of books, eight new Dr. Nurse Romances every two months for £8.00, post and
packing free. If I decide not to subscribe, I shall write to you within 10 days. The free books
are mine to keep in any case. I understand that I may cancel my subscription at any time
simply by writing to you. I am over 18 years of age.
Please write in BLOCK CAPITALS.

Name _____

Address _____

_____

_____ Postcode _____

SEND NO MONEY — TAKE NO RISKS

*Remember, postcodes speed delivery Offer applies in UK only and is not valid to
present subscribers Mills & Boon reserve the right to exercise discretion
in granting membership If price changes are necessary you will be noti-
fied Offer expires 31st December 1984*

8DN

EP11P